"How Can You Kiss Me That Way And Not Feel Any...Want?"

Stefan asked Carrie.

She looked at him and her eyes were enormous. "Of course I do."

He was silent for a minute; then, his voice hoarse, he asked gently, vulnerably, "You do?"

"I have control."

"Well, hell." He lifted his arms and dropped them. "How steely is your control?"

She looked over at him and tilted her head back. "Like iron."

He quickly drew a deeply irritated breath of disgust and exhaled immediately. "Yeah. I'll vouch for that."

Dear Reader:

News flash!

The Branigans Are Back!

All of you who have written over the years to say how much you love Leslie Davis Guccione's BRANIGAN BROTHERS will be thrilled and pleased that this rambunctious family is back with *Branigan's Break*.

More Fun from Lass Small!

We start the New Year with a fun-filled *Man of the Month* from one of your favorite writers. Don't miss *A Nuisance*, which is what our man makes of himself this month!

The Return of Diana Mars!

So many readers have wondered, "Where is Diana Mars?" This popular author took a break from writing, but we're excited that she's now writing for Silhouette Desire with *Peril in Paradise*.

Christmas in January!

For those of you who can't get enough of the holidays, please don't let Suzannah Davis's charming *A Christmas Cowboy* get away.

Mystery and Danger...

In Modean Moon's *Interrupted Honeymoon*.

Baby, Baby...

In Shawna Delacorte's *Miracle Baby*.

So start the New Year right with Silhouette Desire!

With all best wishes for a great 1995,

Lucia Macro
Senior Editor

Please address questions and book requests to:
Silhouette Reader Service
U.S.: 3010 Walden Ave., P.O. Box 1325, Buffalo, NY 14269
Canadian: P.O. Box 609, Fort Erie, Ont. L2A 5X3

Lass Small
A NUISANCE

SILHOUETTE *Desire*®
™ Published by Silhouette Books
America's Publisher of Contemporary Romance

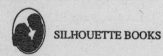 SILHOUETTE BOOKS

ISBN 0-373-05901-9

A NUISANCE

Printed in U.S.A.

Books by Lass Small

Silhouette Desire

Tangled Web #241
To Meet Again #322
Stolen Day #341
Possibles #356
Intrusive Man #373
To Love Again #397
Blindman's Bluff #413
*Goldilocks and the Behr #437
*Hide and Seek #453
*Red Rover #491
*Odd Man Out #505
*Tagged #534
Contact #548
Wrong Address, Right Place #569
Not Easy #578
The Loner #594
Four Dollars and Fifty-One Cents #613
*No Trespassing Allowed #638
The Molly Q #655
+'Twas the Night #684
*Dominic #697
+A Restless Man #731
+Two Halves #743
+Beware of Widows #755
A Disruptive Influence #775
+Balanced #800
+Tweed #817
+A New Year #830
+I'm Gonna Get You #848
+Salty and Felicia #860
+Lemon #879
+An Obsolete Man #895
A Nuisance #901

Silhouette Romance

An Irritating Man #444
Snow Bird #521

Silhouette Books

Silhouette Christmas Stories 1989
"Voice of the Turtles"
Silhouette Spring Fancy 1993
"Chance Encounter"

*Lambert Series
+Fabulous Brown Brothers

LASS SMALL

finds living on this planet at this time a fascinating experience. People are amazing. She thinks that to be a teller of tales of people, places and things is absolutely marvelous.

To three very charming men.

Stan Kulak, who taught me the two Polish sentences.

And the original Stefan Szyszko, who loaned me his name, appearance and allergy to horses.

And our son-in-law Roger Johnson, who wrote the song for our daughter, Liza.

One

—

Stefan Szyszko was a TEXAN, born and bred. From his parents to his great-great-grandparents, the Szyszkos had fit their lives into the town of Blink, near Fredricksburg, TEXAS. When the town was established, it was so small that if you blinked, you missed seeing the town.

Times, population growth and new migrations had changed that, but the name stuck.

While Stefan Szyszko's last name was spelled in that remarkable way, its pronunciation was only subtly different from Cisco which is a very comfortable name in the state of TEXAS. The gently shaded difference could be discerned, and Stefan's ear caught which way he was being addressed.

Stefan Syzszko got a lot of mail addressed to Steve Cisco.

The Szyszkos were Polish. Not just in ancestral roots but in attitude. They were humorous. Their eyes twinkled, their mouths quirked and their laughs were deep and sincere. They were stubborn and independent. They backed what they believed with their talk or fists or their lives.

That probably explains why, in World War II, Germany killed fifteen thousand captive Polish officers, at one time, in one place, deliberately. The Germans knew they couldn't keep the Poles captive. The Polish officers would do their damnedest to escape and fight them again.

All that explained Stefan Szyszko. He was a cheerful, gregarious, stubborn man. He was tall. He stood exactly six feet. He had black hair, which ducktailed. His eyes were blue. He was built like a woman's dream of a man.

He had a rift scar through his right eyebrow. He'd gotten it in a fight over an eleven-year-old girl back when he was about twelve. And in his left earlobe, Stefan wore the plain, wide gold wedding band of his great-grandmother. It balanced the eyebrow scar for the look of a benign pirate.

Nobody had ever seen Stefan really angry. He visited and laughed and gestured and listened. He had one problem. For a TEXAN it was pretty bad. He was allergic to horses.

Pepper Hodges was Stefan's erstwhile good friend who, since puberty, had become his competitor. After Pepper learned of Stefan's allergy, he'd just about always smelled of horses. Then, some of the females had mentioned Pepper always smelled like a horse barn.

Since Pepper was very interested in being close to females, he bathed and changed clothes before any gathering. While it had helped Stefan, it hadn't been for him that Pepper had changed.

So what does a TEXAN do when he's allergic to horses? Stefan had an automobile franchise. Among the Chrysler products, he sold Jeeps. This especially touched his grandfather's heart because he'd used one in Europe in World War II. So nostalgically, he bought a Jeep from his grandson, but he had expected a very large discount.

Bending to kinsmen was one of the debit sides of living in a community that held generations of relatives. Everybody felt they should have a discount on purchases, and they felt free to tell Stefan how to live.

"When are you going to marry?" Stefan's mother asked periodically.

"When I find her," he gave the same, old reply.

"That's not soon enough."

With tested patience, he told his mother, "I'm only thirty."

"Find a good Polish girl and get us some grand-children."

"I'm to look for a baby maker?"

His mother shrugged. "You can find one. A good, sturdy girl with nice, wide hips."

"If I go around measuring hips, I could have trouble with the daddies."

"No. You're such a good catch, the papas would help you measure and cheat with the tape."

Stefan looked patient. He mentioned, "It's possible that hips aren't the most vital part of a marriageable woman."

His mother gave him a side-eyed look and scolded in her humorous nudging, "You want more?"

"Well, her face would have to pass—at least basics."

She waved the idea aside, as if discouraging a nasty fly. "Picky, picky."

Not quite a swear word, he said to his mother, "Dam'd right."

His dad came into the room, and Stefan's mother turned to Stefan's father to complain, "He's looking for a beauty."

Mr. Szyszko raised his eyebrows and looked down his nose at his wife as he replied, "Well, I got one, so why shouldn't he?"

And his wife grinned, tilted up her chin and looked smugly at her son as her head indicated the father. She told the son, "He's smooth. Take lessons."

Stefan figured thirty was too young to get serious. There were too many women to choose from, and all were so delightful that the choosing was an engrossing chore. Well, there were a couple of burrs he'd met, but all the rest were pure delight.

As he drove his new Jeep in the direction of his car lot, his mind came to one of the burrs. She was the most irritating woman God had ever concocted. She worked for the local TV station and was serious about it. She'd be an old maid, a reject. She was already one of his discards.

Ah, but she was something to look at. Her name was Carrie Pierce, and she didn't have the hip measure to please his mother. Carrie was slender. More like a long-legged reed. She had no bosom to speak of, and her hips were narrow. There was no way a man could get a hold on her.

Her hair was strawberry blond. She wore it long, and it was soft and wavy and got tangled up in everything. The wind teased it around so's a man's eyes watched, and his hands would curl for the wanting to get tangled up with her, hair and all.

But the brain under that lure was Carrie's. It was sharp and snotty.

She'd look at a man with those dark brown eyes of hers, and her eyelashes would call attention to themselves in a total lack of modesty. Her brown eyes were like microwave radar, and she would say things like, "What was your car doing at Maggie's the other night?" Just like it was her business to know!

Being a gentleman, he'd respond courteously, "It's none of your business."

And she'd sass "I'll bet," for whatever that meant.

She wasn't even Polish, for crying out loud. Her, with her long, flyaway hair and those narrow hips.

When Stefan's Jeep arrived at the dealership, he looked on the neat, perfectly parked lot with great pride. There were all the little flags lining the elevated wires to call attention to the car lot. The place was spotless. The cars shone in the good TEXAS sunshine. Actually, it was clouding over and about ready to allow the dry TEXAS soil a taste of heavenly moisture.

Stefan drove into his slot and eased himself from his Jeep with great alacrity, easily done with a Jeep. He loved that blunt car. He patted it as he would a good horse, and went into the glass-walled building.

Manny greeted him with, "Kirt Overmann came by for those two Jeeps he ordered."

Stefan asked ominously and with dread, "Did you go over the Jeeps with him like I told you?"

"He was in a hurry."

"Damn it, Manny, I *told* you he'd pull that on you! You were supposed to stall him off and get him to check out each one!"

Earnestly, Manny explained, or complained, "I just couldn't get a word in edgewise."

Scowling, Stefan asked, "Which of the two did he pull?"

"The green one."

Stefan moved his lips around as if rinsing his mouth with a minimum of water, and he guessed, "He'll call just before supper and say the green one doesn't work."

"Leave now."

"I can't. Mac is coming in to make me look at that discard Jeep of his. You know what a pain that'll be?"

Manny comforted his boss. "It isn't even one of ours."

"Try telling him that."

"Show him our file! It isn't there."

Stefan looked at the damned cheerful flags. "He says we snuck the warranty out and burned it."

"You got peculiar friends."

"They're enemies." Stefan sighed. Then he mentioned, "You do recall that Kirt has three marriageable daughters he's trying to palm off on unsuspecting men?"

And Manny's nodding agreement was empathetic.

The phone rang, and Stefan said quickly, "Don't answer it!"

But Manny had already picked it up, and he squinched his face in helpless distress. He had no choice, "Cisco's."

"Steve there?"

Manny's courage only went so far, he said, "Yeah." And he handed the phone to Stefan.

Giving Manny a narrowed-eyed look, Stefan punched the speaker button so Manny could hear both sides. Then he said to the phone, "Stefan here."

And Kirt replied heartily, "Well, hello, Steve, got the Jeeps, but the green one don't want to work. How about coming out and fixing it." A demand.

Stefan looked at his watch. "I can make it about nine-thirty tomorrow morning."

And Kirt asked, "What's pushing you tonight? Everybody 'round owes me, I'll use one of the IOU's to pry you free tonight."

"It's a woman."

There was a pause, and then Kirt asked in a rather deadly way, "Who?"

And right out of his mouth, Stefan lied very stupidly, "Carrie."

Relief rushed through Kirt's, "Carrie? Great! She's here now. You can pick her up...here. Plan on supper." And he hung up.

Stefan slowly, gently recradled the phone. He looked up at Manny's compassionate face and asked, "How many times is it, now, that I'm going to strangle you?"

"Last count? I think I'm down to thirteen."

"Thirteen isn't a lucky count."

"Well, it'll go down lower if you go on out to Kirt's tonight for supper. You got Carrie to protect you from

Kirt's daughters, you can get the green Jeep put back together, eat and sneak away whole."

"You go."

"You know good and well tonight's my night off. You're the boss, and you get to fill in for me." He smiled. "You want me to rescue Carrie? I'd be glad to save her and have her grateful."

"Don't."

Manny then was curious. "What did you have on for tonight that I can help you with?"

And Stefan gave that woman's excuse that covered everything, "I gotta wash my hair."

Manny laughed until he got the hiccups.

Stefan watched stony faced and unamused.

Hiccuping, Manny stood grinning, but with some empathy, he said, "When there was something I had to do that I didn't want to do, my mother always told me, 'It'll grow hair on your chest.' I did more terrible, demanded things than I can count, and look—" he unbuttoned two buttons "—no hair. She lied."

With infinite worldly wisdom, Stefan explained, "It was a figure of speech. She meant the discipline would make a man of you. You need more discipline to reach that goal. Go to Kirt's tonight."

Manny shook a sorrowful head as he said, "God, I'm sure sorry, but I have to go to a funeral."

Stefan narrowed his eyes, his brain going over the obituary columns of the area newspapers in the past week. "Who?"

Gesturing with grandiosity, Manny said, "You, if you interfere with my plans tonight." And he left.

To go to the Overmanns', Stefan didn't shower. He didn't wear his regular clothing. He stripped naked and pulled on some smelly, sweat-and-grease-stained coveralls. He wiped his face and hands with a grease rag. He went in the utility Jeep to Kirt's house on land outside Blink.

He was completely confident that he was safe from being invited into the Overmann house. But dirty, in those grease-stained coveralls and wearing that golden earring, he looked like a potentially dangerous pirate.

The Overmann girls all came out and laughed and flirted while Stefan soberly switched and rearranged wires and connections which had been...switched and rearranged. He didn't make any comment at all about the mess. He just...fixed it back.

Amid the friendly dogs, there was that passel of charming young women, the expansive daddy and the singleton guest named Carrie Pierce. She watched him with almost closed eyes and said nothing at all. She irritated the very hell out of him.

She had on red nail polish. It was daytime. It was too early for her to've gotten dressed for a date. She wore pink polish in the daytime and wore red at night. How come it was daytime and she had on red nail polish?

She had a date that night? Who was he? It wasn't any of Stefan's business. She was a discard. She could go out with any yahoo she wanted to tussle. It was none of his business.

Kirt's wife hollered from the porch, "Get your hands washed, it's about time to eat!"

And Kirt said, "Peel off them coveralls and come on inside. You can finish that up later."

But Stefan had anticipated that very demand and managed a reasonable hesitancy as he looked at the grinning daughters. Helen, Alice and Trisha. Under his breath, Stefan said just for the daddy, "I don't have on nothing else?" That was the TEXAS questioning statement. "This is almost done and— "

In a carrying voice, Kirt exclaimed to the whole community and surrounding area, "You mean to tell me you're nekkid?"

And a genuine blush took over Stefan's face.

The girls giggled, putting their hands to their faces and exchanging laughing glances, but Carrie just watched.

Kirt then said, "No problem. I've got some things you can borrow."

Still working on the mixed-up connections, Stefan next tried a verbal rejection, "I had a late lunch."

"Then you can sit with us for dessert."

Stefan's eyes went reluctantly to see how Carrie was taking all this, and he met her unsympathetic regard. How like her to be aloof when a man was in trouble. No heart. No compassion. No sliver of concern in that icy heart of hers.

He was lucky her strawberry hair hadn't ensnared him. She'd let a man go to the guillotine and never bat those heavily lashed eyelids. She was a mean woman, and he'd made a lucky escape when he'd shunned her.

Then to indicate an unarguable defense, Stefan looked at his cast-off, greasy shoes and shook his head once. "I got to stay outside. Thanks, anyway."

And one of Kirt's pushy daughters said, "We'll all come outside. We'll sit on the porch." And she went to the house to tell her mother.

So her mother hollered for the other girls to come in to help move the meal outside.

Stefan warned them, "It's gonna rain."

And the daughters laughed. "The porch is big enough. You can sit in the rain and get cleaned off."

Snippy. He sorted the daughters out and that one was Helen. He grinned and glanced aside to find Carrie's eyes weighing him.

Why would she do that?

He told that slender, nothing woman with all that blond-red hair, "You'd better get inside. Rain'll melt you."

And wouldn't you know, she had a reply, right away. She said, "I'm not made of sugar."

He was back inside the Jeep's engine, but he did hear her. He mumbled, "I can't argue that."

She asked, "What?"

"I said, 'None of the tires is flat.'" But he pulled his head out of the engine to look at her to see if she believed him, and she laughed.

Those damned brown eyes of hers had all sorts of sparkles in them before those lashes dropped down and hid it all. Asinine woman.

It was Kirt who told Carrie, "Hadn't you better get on home before the storm hits?"

"I was invited to dinner before Stefan got here. If there isn't enough to include us both, he can leave."

Stefan relaxed. "Yeah."

"Or he can follow me home, to be sure I get there in this wild and woolly storm that's going to spray us with a few sprinkles."

Kirt narrowed his eyes and considered her.

Stefan said, "With the storm coming, you probably ought to get on home. I'll follow you and come back tomorrow and finish this up."

Kirt broke in. "No. You stay. We promised you dessert. You can't wiggle out of that. We're having Mildred's pe-can pie."

Stefan groused, "No! Good thing I've already eaten. Her pie is so good I'll have to have two pieces."

The father put in, "The girls all can make that pie. They're good cooks."

Stefan thought what a touter Kirt was. He'd get those girls married off—but not to Stefan. He went back to working on rescuing the tangled connections.

Kirt said, "Give it up for now. It's about to rain."

"I don't have much more to do. I'll get it done. Go ahead. I'll be quick. Carrie, you hold the flashlight."

Kirt said, "No. I will."

Stefan countered, "You need to clean up a little before you go inside Mildred's pristine house. You know that fc˙ a fact."

And Kirt knew it. "We'll fix you a place. Come along, Carrie."

But Stefan told Kirt, "She's gotta hold the flashlight."

There was nothing Kirt could do about that. He had to go inside. His daughters were all inside the house, helping their mother. Carrie was the only one left outside to hold the light for Stefan. Damn!

Kirt gave Carrie's slender body a look and was reassured. It was just her hair. Nothing else on her could lure a man, and he knew that Stefan was immune to her. So he turned away. "Don't be long." And Kirt left.

As soon as he was out of earshot, that nasty Carrie giggled.

Stefan chided, "Shame on you."

"Hush. Don't say another word, or I'll leave you here and go on home."

Stefan groused, "That's just exactly what you'd think of doing. You're a witch!"

"You've said something like that before."

"I never!"

She was emphatic, "When I wouldn't stay the night with you."

"Shame on you, saying that kind of thing about a nice young man like me."

"You're past thirty." She pointed that out like he hadn't known such a fact. "You're supposed to be a responsible man."

"I'm getting this damned motor rewired. That's really taking responsibility the hard way."

She was flippant. "So's behaving yourself."

"You weren't interested."

She didn't say anything.

He lifted his head up and looked at her across the engine. "You're a damned tease."

She didn't respond.

"You're lucky I didn't wring your neck."

She was silent.

The rain started gently.

He said, "Go on inside. I can finish this in just a minute."

The flashlight held steady.

He told her, "You're going to get wet."

And her husky, wicked voice replied, "I've already told you that I won't melt."

"You won't. You're hard-hearted and mean. There isn't anything on this earth that would make you pliant."

And her laugh was low and soft.

* * *

It wasn't long before Stefan wiped his hands on his greasy coveralls. He went to the Jeep and slid onto the newspaper Kirt had insisted on putting across the driver's seat. The Jeep started like it'd never had a problem, and Stefan gave a huge sigh of endurance.

He turned off the ignition, got out of the Jeep and looked at Carrie. He said, "You can turn off the flashlight. We're through. You're good help. Thank you."

She didn't reply. She just turned off the light and went over to put it in the glove compartment.

The initial rain was gentle. TEXAS rain was just about always like that, so as the ground wouldn't be too shocked with the coming wetness. Stefan lifted his face to it.

In the dusk's light rain, Stefan stood in his messed-up coveralls, with that earring and the rifted eyebrow. He looked more like a pirate than ever. Carrie licked her lips.

From the house, Kirt hollered, "Hustle up, you all, we're just about finished!"

"Coming." Stefan said the word so they could hear him on the porch, but he was looking at Carrie.

She smiled faintly. She was very alert and her eyes went over him in quick moves.

Stefan closed the Jeep up and wiped his hands on the already greasy rag in his hip pocket. He gestured and said, "Ladies first."

She lifted her eyebrows slightly and mentioned, "Lady? The last time I heard you refer to me, you called me a cold — — — — —."

He slid his narrowed eyes over her and replied, "I was being polite."

She tilted her head and regarded him. "Polite? Then . . . or now."

But Kirt hollered, "Hustle up!"

Sitting under the roof of the overhang by the porch, Stefan ate two quarters of one pie. It was delicious, and Mildred insisted he take the rest of it home. She smiled and told him, "Helen did this one."

Helen laughed with such humor that Stefan knew the mother lied.

Although the host insisted he'd follow Carrie home to be sure she was safe—in that isolated, pure, staid area—he couldn't argue when Stefan explained Carrie was going in his direction and her house came first.

So the marriageable daughters and their papa all went out to supervise the separate ones in getting into their cars and leaving the Overmann place.

Kirt was at Stefan's Jeep, talking, as Stefan waited for the sisters to finish their farewells to Carrie. They'd been talking since last night, apparently, but they *still* had things to say . . . and things to laugh about.

Finally, finally Carrie eased her car along, and the sisters walked along to finish one more hysterical comment. Carrie eased her way with the sisters bending over and touching one another in their hilarity.

As he followed Carrie, Stefan wondered, What was so funny?

With dispatch, the cold witch drove perfectly down the road, staying on her side of it, not nudging the speed limit, driving perfectly. Women were such an irritation.

Deliberately sagged down in his seat, Stefan lagged along. Keeping her in sight, he was looking around just wishing some yahoo would harass her. And he could go to her rescue and sort things out.

Now...why on this earth would he want something like that to happen?

He moved his mouth around as he mentally chewed on such a stupid wish. He supposed it was because she was so damned confident that, at almost twenty-three, she felt she was more mature than him.

They entered the town of Blink from one side and drove through residential streets. From some distance, he saw her turn between the cement posts at the entrance of the Pierce driveway and park her car by the back door. She got out and immediately went into the house.

He leisurely swung his car between those same cement posts and into her drive...as the back house light went out.

She hadn't waited to thank him for his escort.

Her parents were out of town. Her brother was in grad school. Carrie was alone in the house.

He pulled his car up in back of hers and got out with great, enduring patience. He went up on her screened back porch's steps and pounded his fist, rattling the wooden frame of the screen door.

He heard the upstairs shower turn on.

Now, she *had* to've heard his Jeep. She *had* to've heard the Jeep door slam. She *had* to've heard his feet clunk on the back wood steps. And she *had* to've heard his knock on the loose, although hooked screen door. He knew it was hooked because it had not opened to his tug.

So he sat in the mist, on the steps, and waited. When the upstairs shower finally turned off, some time later, he swung his fist around and really rattled that door.

After a time, he repeated the rattle.

She came to the kitchen door that led onto the screened porch. She was dressed in a bathrobe that buttoned under her chin, and said, "Some problem with your Jeep?"

Still sitting on her back steps, he replied, "You got inside before I knew nobody had accosted you. How'd I know the sound of the shower wasn't a cover-up of a ravishing?"

In a dead voice with no emphasis at *all*, she replied, "Glory be."

"You're not only cold, you're mouthy."

"Yeah."

He said grudgingly, "Thank you for the protection you gave me tonight at the Overmanns'." The words were wooden, but along with an eye-rolling sigh, his mother would've been proud of him.

But that nasty, mostly blond redhead said with greatly exaggerated candor, "What was threatening you out at the Overmanns'? On the way here? How did I help you? You're allergic to water...the rain? Why don't you get back in your Jeep and get out of the rain?"

He gave her a slow turning of his head and a withering look that should have shriveled her. It did not. Then he rose and stretched his tired muscles. He breathed the misting air before he took his own sweet time going back to the Jeep and leaving her standing there, in her doorway, watching after him.

But as he was slowly backing down her driveway, he heard her phone ringing.

Some poor dolt was trying for her. Stupid guy. It never entered Stefan's mind that the caller might be female. He only thought of some guy talking in her ear in a low and intimate way and...trying.

Sourly, he drove on to his car lot. He went around, being sure it was all secure... followed by the patient security guard, Tad.

Tad said, "Mac was here. He thinks you're avoiding him. That you won't face your responsibilities."

"Do you know how long he's had that Jeep? He got it at a post World War II government auction."

"He says it was here."

"I wasn't alive then. This was grazing land at that time. I don't sell used Jeeps. Nobody gives them up."

"He's allowing you that privilege."

"Tad. This has not been a good day. Kirt bought two Jeeps and got away with them before Manny or I could go over them with him. Do you realize how many times I'm gonna have to go out yonder to his place... just before supper?"

Tad smiled.

"Tad... would you go th—"

"I'm tagged. Eula wouldn't allow me to set foot on Kirt's property. She's a hellcat." His voice was benign and a bit smug.

Stefan gave him a slow and deadly look. "I hate a bragging man."

"You need a permanent woman. She'll be nice to you. She'll guard you from other women. You can tell her now isn't the best time to get it legal."

"You're smarter'n me." Stefan looked glumly out over the darkening night fall over the TEXAS land. The rain was a benediction. How could he be so glum? At his age and circumstance, he should be carefree and jubilant. He ought to be able to peel off those coveralls and go out and romp in the gentle rain, glorying in being alive and free.

Everywhere he looked, there were traps.

Two

Stefan turned away from his night watchman, Tad. He walked toward his Jeep. He was ready to leave his car lot and said his usual comment, "Watch."

So his night watchman replied with great patience, "Hell, man, I do. That's why you hired me. Me and Tom are good watchers."

Stefan frowned at the placid dog. "I knew of a watchdog in Florida who did only that. He would watch as the whole kaboodle was stolen."

"You're offending him." Tad indicated his alert dog.

Stefan placated, "Naw. Saying 'watch' is just automatic. My mother still tells me to 'be careful' every time I leave their house, after visiting."

"Mine just says 'behave.' I wonder who's spilling her guts to my momma."

"Nobody. Mothers set traps."

"Yeah." After a thoughtful silence, Tad inquired, "If your mother says that, what's your dad say?"

Stefan gestured to indicate grand wisdom. "He said that to deal with a Polish man, American women need only two sayings in Polish."

"What's that?" Tad looked interested.

"*Idz do piekla* and *jacie kocham*."

"What's that mean?"

"'Go to hell' and 'I love you.' Those two sayings will cover any situation. In conversation, a woman needs only to listen."

Tad laughed.

Stefan again started for his Jeep. "Watch."

"Hell, man, we just went through all that."

"Yeah." And Stefan finally left.

As he drove along, he studied his restlessness. Why? Well, it seemed to him that a whole lot of nothings got in the way of his life.

Look at Kirt fooling with the innards of a new car because he had three marriageable daughters. Or his own mother's anxiety over his single life. There was that stupid, old man, Mac, claiming Stefan was responsible for an antique government-issue Jeep finally groaning with age. And then there was the damned woman with the blond-red hair who was so cool and collected . . . but not by him.

Now why had he thought of Carrie as a problem of *his?* He'd discarded her three months ago. She was a holdout and pigheaded and impossible.

Impossible was sure true. Any woman who'd kiss like that, and then say no, was mean! Think what a woman like that would do with little kids! She'd rule with an iron hand. "Eat that spinach!" "It's bedtime. You get yourself right upstairs. This is the last time I'm telling you!" "You play hookey and I'll blister you!" She'd be relentless.

She'd probably want more Polish words than just "go to hell." She'd tongue-lash a good man.

But then he began a dreamy vision of her tongue-lashing him, here and there, and he lost all his hostility. He'd be putty in her seeking hands. She'd turn him into a slave. He'd starve, waiting for her attentions.

It was just a good thing he'd wiped her from his mind and excluded her from his life.

On the other side of Blink, out where Stefan lived, there were no sidewalks. There were wire fences along the road. And the county didn't mow the sides of the road, so the weeds were high outside the fence. His "yard" was somewhat mowed, but there was no trimming done. It was all pretty weedy and loose. Casual? It suited Stefan.

However, the house was plumb and painted, and so was the garage and shed in back of it. There was also a neat outhouse, just in case. Across the back of the house was a great, open screened porch, a lot like the ones other people had.

Inside, the furnishings were family castoffs. He did have a new bed, a good refrigerator, stove and a dishwasher. He did not wash dishes by hand.

He looked over the place and it was his.

When he got out of his car, the phone rang. That surprised him. It was almost ten, and people went to bed early in Blink. He went into the unlocked house and picked up the receiver with some curiosity.

Her tongue said, "You got home okay?"

He took a satisfied breath and began to sit down to talk as he said, "Yeah."

But the witch hung up.

Why the hell had she called? She was paying him back for him making sure she'd gone into the house safely?

Tit for tat.

That only set his mind off again.

He went through his sparsely furnished house and up the stairs into his bedroom. Upstairs, his bedroom was the only furnished room. Stefan went to the shower and used the liquid soap to get rid of the remainder of the grease. Then he put on clean pajama pants and faced the fact that there wasn't much else to do but go to bed.

So he did.

And the next thing he knew, he awoke to the alarm. His bed was a torn-up mess, and he was not rested.

So what was the problem? He sure as hell didn't need more exercise.

He lay in his silent room in the silent house and went over his potential conversation with Mac, who was eighty-two, a childless widower and lonely. Stefan's dad's solution was to just go ahead and give Mac a new Jeep.

At that time, Stefan had replied, "Hell, Dad, if I did that, every yahoo in the county would come a-running, declaring their Jeep was one of mine, defective and needed to be replaced."

So his dad had said, "For Mac's Jeep, make it seem like a competition. It might cost you a Jeep or two, but it would salve that old man's heart. He's lonely. Why don't you hire him as a salesman?"

"I thought I was supposed to hire Carrie."

His dad had agreed. "Her, too. She'd draw men in like they're flies after honey."

"I can't submit her to that sort of harassment."

His dad had slid his eyes over to his youngest son and inquired, "Jealous?"

"I gave up on her over three months ago."

"When was that?"

"Dad, you're pushing it."

His dad had shrugged. "We like her."

"Which 'we'? Are you implying Momma likes her?"

"You and me."

Stefan had reminded his gene contributor, "Momma called her a tart."

His dad had soberly nodded agreement. "It was the dress. It was like a second skin."

"So you did notice. I thought you told Momma you hadn't seen it."

His dad had gestured openly. "There are just times when a man's better off temporarily blind."

"Now you tell me."

"Hell, Stef, I've told you that 'til I'm blue in the face! Just look!"

Stefan looked his dad over quite critically, because he was feeling critical. He said, "Your face's pretty pink. There's a blood vessel there that looks busted."

"That was from the night you first took out the car, alone, with that youngest Sorrus girl."

Stefan had sighed and shaken his head in empathy for a lousy time. "I remember that."

"I should hope you would!"

Stefan had to remind his father, "It's stuck in my head because I had to go and get her daddy to get his mules to haul us out of the sand."

"That did take guts."

"It was the car," Stefan again vowed. "I couldn't allow my first car to sink in quicksand."

"But you left her inside the car," his father had retorted in a censorious manner. "I've never understood that."

"I told you. She had on high heels, and I didn't want to wait around for her to make the trek. She was fifteen. She wobbled in high heels on a smooth surface. What if somebody else had come along, pulled the car out and took it off. I figured if she stayed in it, the car was still mine."

"And if it sunk?"

"Dad." Stefan had been very adult. "All this happened fourteen years ago."

"You asked about my burst blood vessel."

"No." Stefan had then managed to be excruciatingly patient. "I just barely mentioned it. You asked if your face was blue from giving me sage advice."

"Sage? You a horticulturist?"

That had done it. In order to avoid a burst blood vessel of his own then, Stefan had said, "Tell Momma I was here."

"Probably."

That one word had caused Stefan to hesitate on his way to the door. "Why...probably?"

"I'll have to test how she's feeling about you, before I admit you was here."

"Do you realize there are people that have real, normal parents? How'd I end up with you two?" Then, hopefully, he'd asked rapidly, "Was I adopted?"

"No. You're ours."

"That's scary." And Stefan had left.

* * *

Stefan had four brothers. They were a year apart in age. Stefan was youngest. His mother had told Stefan that when he was born, and she was exhausted and groggy, his father had told her—at that time, mind you—that he'd finally figured out how to have daughters. Even Stefan's father admitted that he could have chosen a better time for his pronouncement. His wife didn't speak kindly to him for two years.

So why did Stefan think Carrie would be any different? She was also a touchy female, just like his mother. Well. Why was he interested in Carrie who was a rejected woman? It was that hair. And disgruntled, he thought about the fact that everybody has hair. Well, someplace on them. There aren't very many people who are bald all over. But Carrie had all that mop of shimmery blond-strawberry hair. It was alluring. A man wanted to be wrapped in it.

He decided he'd casually mention to her that some of the men at his place had talked about the fact that she'd look better with her hair cut short. If she cut it, he figured, it ought to solve his lured-attention problem.

Then, more than likely, she'd mention something he should cut. Like his own throat.

When he came back into his house the next time, the phone was ringing, and it was that woman, Carrie, who said, "You get home okay?"

He didn't sit down that time, he just said, "Yeah."

"Who all did you accost?"

So he eased down and heard himself saying, "Some guys out at the lot were talking about you."

"Naturally."

She was snippy and just asking for some man to take charge of her and straighten her out. He went on, "And they think you'd look cute with your hair real short. I told them they were crazy."

She hung up.

Several days passed and just about everyone in Blink heard of the scam Stefan's dad had contrived. Stefan was going to give away a new Jeep in exchange for one from the time of World War II. Ownership had to've been continuous.

The idea was attention-getting. Stefan would actually trade a new Jeep for an antique. But it was worth doing because of the publicity.

Mac did win. The two runners-up each got a hundred dollars.

Kirt said thoughtfully, "Mac's old Jeep up on a pole out front of the car lot would be a plus. Up in the air, thataway, it would be seen from the highway."

It is odd what happenstance does. While Stefan was just trying to get Mac off his neck, the newspapers from around the area clear to San Antonio, up to Austin and over to Fredricksburg came for interviews with Stefan . . . and pictures!

Those combatants left from World War II were getting precious. World War II had been a "good" war. It wasn't like the newer wars, so nasty and appalling.

Memory is selective.

Stefan had never had such publicity. It was good for business. He gave a second Jeep to his father.

Was his father delighted? No. He said furiously, "What the hell you trying to do? You want me to look like a moocher?" And he refused the Jeep.

Stefan begged God to prove he was switched at birth. Or at least adopted!

As he drove around the area for television interviews, he dreamed his real parents would recognize him and claim him. He hadn't dreamed that since he was fourteen, just over half his life ago.

Then he heard by chance that Carrie had all his TV interviews taped! The very thought of her watching him on tape wobbled him. Why would she tape the interviews?

But he overheard his father say, "Our VCR went crazy and chewed up tapes, but Carrie volunteered to tape the TV bits on Stefan for us. She has a double VCR that can hold twelve hours of—"

The sound of his daddy's voice went away, and Stefan's head was filled with the popping air waves of a vacuum. It was fascinating. Eventually, he was aware that the stunning reason for his mental vapidness was the fact that Carrie would volunteer to tape his interviews for his parents!

Did that mean . . . Did she have copies?

His father's voice came back to Stefan. "We don't even have to watch or fool with the recorder. They give Carrie the day, channel and hour, and she just sets the time and so on. She really doesn't mind, it's so simple."

Stefan was deflated. She didn't have to watch the tapes. She just programmed the VCR. That sobered him.

Why had he been . . . un-sobered? Why had his libido gotten so excited when he heard she was . . . But she wasn't. She was simply being kind to his parents.

Yeah. And just why was she being kind to his parents? Hmm?

His head waggled a little, his body moved a bit and he touched his tie. Carrie Pierce was interested in Stefan Szyszko?

He could understand it. After he dumped her, she hadn't been able to get over him. She was courting his parents to get through to him. She was trying to get them on her side and trap him. Yeah.

At church the next Sunday, Stefan watched in some shock as Carrie came inside with Pepper Hodges. What the *hell* was she doing with Pepper, of all men? And why was she with him . . . in church!

And Stefan knew. Just that fast, it came to him. Pepper was the fall guy. She wanted to see Stefan. And she wanted him to see her with another man and get territorial. Yep.

Knowing all that, he wasn't surprised when she didn't look around to find him. He sat there with his parents, three of his brothers and their families, in a Szyszko fortress of relations, and he knew that she knew right where he was.

When had she gotten that big, floppy hat? It looked really good on that skinny, shapeless woman. She had good taste. And she was there, in church, with Pepper Hodges. She was lucky she was in church with a guy like that. She'd better be careful.

How come she had paired off with Pepper? Well, she didn't belong to that church. Coming with Pepper was the only way she could seem normal when she came inside. But she still didn't look around. How did she know he would know she would be with Pepper?

And Stefan figured it out. She'd come in during the week and checked the pews for names. Yeah. She had. She knew where he was. He relaxed and studied the

statue of Jesus showing his cross-impaled heart
wrapped in thorns, and Stefan felt great compassion.

When the service was over, and they were moving
out of the church, Stefan saw that Carrie and Pepper
were ahead of him. It seemed odd that she would allow that. She should have waited until he exited the
church and was standing around outside as he talked,
then she could have come out and been surprised to see
him.

She wasn't handling a confrontation at all well. But
she was a novice. She'd learn.

However, she had taped his interviews. He would be
kind to mention his mother's gratitude. He'd be casual about it. He squeezed through impossible barri-
ers of talking people, knocked a lady's hat askew and
walked through empty pews and got outside just in
time to see her being put into Pepper's car!

What was the rush?

And a thought stopped him cold. What if... what
if she was allowing Pepper to... court her!

Yeah. What if?

And he found he was stunned by the idea. His mind
rejected it. How could he be so upset over a woman
whom he'd discarded three months and seventeen days
ago?

How come he knew exactly how long ago it had
been?

Was he sulking? Had he been waiting for her to call
him and make up with him, saying he was right and
she'd been rude? Yeah.

So what was he supposed to do?

* * *

Knowing her family was still away, Stefan called her the rest of the day, and fortunately she didn't have the pushy answering machine connected. Each time, he could let the phone ring twenty times. If she deliberately was not answering, it would be annoying for her to have to listen to the long rings, but he knew she wasn't there. No single woman would resist a ringing phone.

When he couldn't contact her the next day, he began to get a breathing disorder. Where was she? How could he find out without seeming interested? A man's life and times were a heavy burden.

He drove by her house, using different cars from the lot so he could be anonymous. Sure. But he went by the next night and her driveway was filled with cars. She was having a party, and he hadn't been invited?

He was crushed. It was several days before he found out her visitors had been sorority sisters. Finding that out kept him from going into a decline. But...why would he care?

Then Pat Vernon called. He was one of the people from the TV station in San Antonio who had interviewed Stefan. Pat had called because Mac's earpiece didn't accept the telephone. Pat had found a World War II veteran who was only sixty-eight and he could still qualify to fly a single-engine plane.

His name was Jerold Kraut. It would be good copy if Mac would go on a flight with Jerold. Pat asked Stefan, "Would you find out if Mac would be interested? We can land the plane right behind your car lot. It'd give you some free publicity."

Stefan said, "Great. Why don't you come out and talk to the old man with me."

"Is there a motel around there? I don't recall one in Blink."

"You can stay with me? I have the room. Mac'll come into town, and it'll probably be fun. My mother will fix the meals and you can't get any better than that."

"You talked us into it. What day?"

So they got that figured out.

Stefan's father and a couple of his brothers helped him move an extra bed out of the family storage in the barn. The struggle to put it into one of the vacant rooms at Stefan's house was so difficult that it was hilarious, and they became weak from laughing. Then they decided they might just as well put a bed in the other room. So Stefan bought a case of beer.

His mother told Stefan to buy some mattress covers so the stains wouldn't show. She loaned him sheets and towels. And pillows. And dishes. And she donated two braided rugs. She told him that if he put one end under the bed no one would notice the indelible stains on one of the rugs. And she added a rocking chair to set on the stubborn stain on the other rug.

Stefan said, "That's the rocker you used for feeding us kids."

His mother looked at it critically. "It'll last."

Slipping it in slyly, Stefan offhandedly asked his mother, "Can we come to your house at mealtime? Just supper." He gestured as if that was no big deal, and "just supper" was letting her off the hook.

She was agreeable, but she gave Stefan a look, and he knew she was collecting brownie points. She'd hit him with some god-awful job for him to solve, and he would be committed to it. The weight of that reality came down and landed heavily on his shoulders.

Carrying the burden of probable obligation, Stefan checked with the area weatherman. He said the weather ought to be okay for the next several weeks, and to check back.

In an afterthought, Stefan finally had to go see Mac because he couldn't talk to him on the phone. Mac was willing to be involved in the filming. By then, Stefan wouldn't have been at all surprised if the old geezer had flatly refused. Stefan's confidence in himself wasn't high.

But then Mac hesitated. "You say the pilot's not even seventy? A whippersnapper. You suppose he'll know what the hell he's doing? What'd you say? Don't mumble, boy."

Therefore, it was a real fluke that Stefan had a valid excuse to call Carrie. She wasn't at the TV station, but she was home.

Before she could reject his call, he said, "I wonder if you'd be kind enough to set your VCRs to tape another string of great promo coverage." He just went ahead and told her what and when and why.

She said a calm, "Sure. No problem. I'll contact your mother for the times."

"I'll make a list and bring it to you."

"No need." She rejected seeing him. "You'll be busy."

"Carrie."

"Yes?"

Quite serious and deliberately vulnerable, he told her, "I'd like you to be my guest for this. Would you?"

"I'm very busy."

"Please."

There was a long silence. He resisted any of the crowding questions that he sweat over, like: Were she and Pepper sleeping together? Was she totally finished with Stefan Szyszko? Could she bring herself to be with him even just one or two days? He wanted her filmed with him, if the film crew did that.

She said, "I suppose."

"You photograph so well, you'll be the star."

"Why Stefan Szyszko, you're a gentleman!"

"I'm sure as hell trying." And his breath caught in his chest over his own unexpected words. What was he saying?

She waited then said, "Call me when the schedule is solid."

"Why don't I pick you up now and we can figure where it's best for the plane to land and take off?"

She laughed low and very amused.

Since he was dead serious, he wasn't aware of anything except that she hadn't hung up on him, yet.

Carrie's voice said in his ear, "Now, how will we know something like that?"

And his tricky mind supplied, "We can figure how the wind blows and how we can get the takeoffs and landings with the car lot in the background."

"Smart. Ask the pilot."

Unhappily, his stupid tongue then demanded, "What were you doing in church with Pepper Hodges?"

Just like that, she replied, "I was so surprised to see you there that I was a total blank."

His voice went low and velvety. "So you knew I was there."

"The other people all looked like good churchgoers...then there was you. You tend to stand out in any crowd, but you are a sore thumb in a church."

He was offended. "Why?"

"You look like what most women are praying about."

"To get me?"

And her voice was soft and gentle. "To get away from you." And she quietly hung up.

Thoughtfully serious, Stefan laid his phone gently in its cradle. He was sober and pensive. She wanted to get away from him. Why?

So he went into a period of grief. He was being shunned. He forgot all about having discarded her...so recently. He only knew she felt he was unsuitable and therefore a man for a woman to escape. His opinion of himself wavered.

His mother recognized his conduct. She was kind and gentle with her youngest. His brothers were roughnecks and laughed at him, but the fact he didn't notice their abrasive humor caused them to ask their parents, "What's eatin' the shrimp?"

Their father replied, "Let up on him."

And their mother said, "Leave him alone."

So his brothers knew it was something serious. They made inquiries about his car business and learned he was doing great. They discussed his health and it was okay. So it had to be a woman, but they couldn't figure out which one. He'd discarded the strawberry blonde.

They took him hunting, and scoffed at him and needled him and razed him so that he would feel loved.

And in case the problem was a reluctant woman, they mentioned that they envied him for being single and loose.... They told about all the times they'd been turned down, and they made it hilarious.

It was a great time. Then without shooting a rifle but with the beer gone, they went home. The brothers felt they'd been indispensable. Stefan would be okay, since he knew he had four brothers and they backed him.

Stefan hadn't really noticed.

The time came when Pat Vernon, the producer from the San Antonio TV station, came to Blink to plot the flight. The television crew came along. They invaded Stefan's house as if it was their own. And they groused at the cameraperson, who was a slender brunette woman. She didn't budge from wanting a bedroom to herself. Selfish. They had all been unselfishly willing to share. She was just another stubborn woman.

That gave Stefan a perfect excuse to call Carrie and ask, "We have a woman cameraperson here—" He allowed that to soak in. "She insists on sleeping alone, using all of one of the bedrooms. Would you be kind enough to get her out of our hair?"

Stefan was that unkind because he wanted Carrie to understand he couldn't be lured by another woman. While he recognized his motive, he didn't examine it at all.

"Tell her to come on over."

"Well, she doesn't have a car."

"I'll come fetch her," Carrie volunteered. "She can use mine."

"What'll you do?"

"Pepper has a sp—"

And Stefan's speech tromped on *any*thing Pepper might be able to do. Stefan said in a hurry, "You can have one of the spare cars." And he was exuberant! She'd be driving one of his cars! His smile spread over his face.

But Carrie mentioned logically, "Just lend a Jeep to the woman."

Stefan was appalled. "Uh. She can't drive a Jeep."

"I thought you said even a little child can drive one."

"She's stupid," he hurriedly told Carrie. "She needs a basic car."

"Mine is not automatic. Can she shift gears?"

"Yes." Stefan had to admit it.

"Then let her use the Jeep."

His mind racing, Stefan blurted, "I don't trust her with one of my good Jeeps and—"

"Stefan," Carrie was extraordinarily patient. "If you wouldn't trust this strange female with your Jeep, then why should I lend her my car?"

"I'll get back to you." Then he added hurriedly, "Thank you for taking her in. The guys need two rooms. She was selfish. Just like—" And he stopped.

"Just...like...what?" Carrie's voice was deadly.

His Baltic Sea, Polish pirate genes replied without his permission, "Just like you." And he gently hung up on her exclamation.

He sat silently, trying to sort out how he was to handle this woman. Carrie. It was not a Polish name. It was from the British Isles. No wonder he was having so much trouble with her. The Irish had been there first and the British were still having trouble controlling them. Stefan understood the frustration of the British.

But his Polish blood understood the Irish. Poles disliked being pushed or dominated.

Then Stefan tried to think of any people who willingly submitted to another, and he came up without any race who would.

And then there were women and men. Men were in an endless struggle to try to control females. It was just about impossible. But men were tenacious and they would survive and dominate.

Fat chance.

Three

The brunette cameraperson's name was Minnie Tombs, but a couple of the guys called her Many Times and snickered a lot.

There are just males who are slow to mature.

Minnie was enduring. Since Szyszko didn't harass her, she looked at him with some interest, until she saw how he looked at Carrie.

Minnie and Carrie hit it off from the first glance. Carrie was that way. She fitted in with other women very easily.

Watching the two, Stefan thought he'd just made a very formidable mistake, allowing that cameraperson into Carrie's house and into Carrie's control. He considered them and frowned.

The men bached it at Stefan's. The eighty-two-year-old Mac fit into the male household with ex-military ease. He was the only one who had a room alone.

He'd been a master sergeant in World War II. Everybody knows a master sergeant has things the way he wants them, and he didn't cotton to sharing a room with any other male.

Stefan had to share his room with Pat and one of the other men, and those who were left took over the third bedroom. At night, the snoring was really something.

As usual with new people, the guests were fascinated with Stefan's last name. That started when one of them said, "You have a good TEXAS name... Cisco."

Just the pronunciation showed the name was wrong. Stefan replied, "I'm Polish. My last name's spelled different."

"Yeah?"

So Stefan spelled his name and that threw them all for a loop. "What!"

The owner of the Polish name was practiced in his patience with the uninitiated.

Stefan and the crew, plus Minnie, would be out for days looking over backgrounds for filming, but they spent suppertime and the evenings at the Szyszkos'.

Besides helping with setting the table and the clearing away and dishwashing, the photo crew was primarily learning how to spell the Szyszko name, and complaining because the Szyszko parents hadn't had daughters.

That brought up Mr. Szyszko's telling his wife about him finally knowing how to make girls just after his fifth son was born. The guys loved the story; Stefan's mother was patient.

About that time, Carrie brought Minnie and some other women along, and the guys got polite and careful.

Mrs. Szyszko mentioned the quietness to her husband, and he explained, "Women terrify men."

She scoffed.

He was surprised, "Haven't you ever noticed how careful and quiet I am around you?"

She gasped, too quickly.

Then the guests wanted to know why Mrs. Szyszko was choking. "What's the matter?"

Patting her back, Mr. Szyszko replied, "I shocked her."

"What did you say?" They were concerned.

"Something obviously too adult for you kids."

They objected their youth, and they all made suggestions on how to stop Mrs. Szyszko's coughing. "Pat her back."

"Raise her arm up."

"No, the left one. Higher."

They sought to distract her. They played like apes and made strange noises and tried to scare her—the mother of five sons—but she only coughed harder.

Mr. Szyszko instructed, "You *scare* hiccups!" But he took his wife out of the room.

It was only then that Stefan realized Carrie had cut off just about *all* of her magical hair! He was stunned. She'd done that?

He stared at her. And in all that bedlam, she slid her eyes over and returned his stare. Then she turned away from him and rejoined the chattering laughter.

With Mrs. Szyszko gone from the room, Pat Vernon suggested to Minnie, "Hiccup. We'll figure out a way to scare you."

She was used to them and declined the entertainment.

Pat chided, "You're selfish."

Stefan thought that exactly identified Carrie. She'd selfishly kept her body to herself and now she'd cut off her hair. How come he hadn't noticed that right away? He hadn't because she was magical. A man was so stunned by her aura that he didn't immediately notice detail. She'd cut off her hair!

No man should get involved with a woman like her. And he watched her through slitted eyes as she laughed and hushed and chided the teasing men.

They were after her. They had no chance at all. Then . . . why was she laughing thataway?

Stefan strolled casually over and positioned himself beside Carrie. He would protect her. She was not alone. He was there. He proceeded to give various males his deadly, narrow-eyed *cut it out right now* look.

They ignored him.

Stefan sighed. He'd obviously never appeared to be the formidable threat he knew he was.

When Carrie tried to leave his side, Stefan took her arm in his hand and asked through clenched teeth, "Why'd you cut off your hair?"

She carelessly rumpled what was left. It was thick and ducktailed charmingly under her hands, but her mouth said . . . she actually *said*, "You told me to."

He gasped in indignation! But at the same time, he clearly remembered goading her with the false statement that the guys had all said she ought to cut her hair.

So she had!

Women were excruciatingly stupid.

She smiled at him and said, "See? Is this better?" And she had the gall to wait for his reply.

Stefan was stilled by appalled shock! The other men heard her question and got to crowd around her and touch her head and ruffle her hair, what was left of it. But Stefan was unable to move or comment because he was still in the speechless, staring stage.

With Carrie's hair cut off that way, attention was drawn to her luscious body. The men had always stared at her body, but then they could alibi, "Her hair is really something." And they discussed and touched her hair, but they looked at the rest of her.

Under the jocular byplay of the mob, Stefan could quietly ask the wicked woman, "You drawing attention to yourself?"

"Not that I'm aware."

"You cut your hair so's men would notice your body?"

She looked down at her gorgeously refined shape and had the sass to question, "This old thing?" But she glanced up at him and her eyes were serious and rather cold.

He shivered.

So she asked, "What's the matter with you?"

"You're freezing me out."

She tilted back her head and said through her teeth, right there in his parents' living room, "You discarded me."

"When?"

She stopped her tongue, which was about to give the exact day count, before she replied, "Some time ago."

Stefan frowned and squinted as he tried to recall doing any such thing. "I don't recall doing anything like that."

"You did. You walked out on me and you shut the door."

She turned and left him in the silent room where people were laughing and gesturing and enjoying each other's humor. Stefan was alone in a vacuum.

How was he to recapture her attention? She didn't answer her phone. She wouldn't talk to him. She was snippy and aloof. How could he reach her?

Women were a pushover for any injury. He needed to bleed. His parents' house had been an injury-proof haven since their first son was born. Now, how could Stefan get a wound there? He signaled Jeff with a backward move of his head. His friend came over.

Stefan took Jeff's arm and moved out of the mainstream of people. He told Jeff, "I need to bleed a little. How about hitting me on my face."

"What?" Jeff stopped moving and looked at Stefan in some shock.

Stefan was impatient. "I need to bleed. Hit my nose, but don't break it. You got finesse. You can do this."

"Now, Stef, you and I've been buddies since kindergarten? How would it look if I did something like that to you at this point? Here in your parents' house? What excuse could I give?"

And Stefan remembered that Jeff had always been a stickler. Stefan looked around for another friend who wasn't so structured.

One guy asked, "Whose attention are you trying for?" And he'd looked around. In one scanning of the room, he had it. "Carrie. I can understand that, but she might get mad at me and tell Karen."

One told Stefan, "Don't be so stupid. What did you do to offend her? Apologize and give her a great, big, impossible floral arrangement that'll boggle her."

And another replied, "Don't be any more stupid than whatever caused your breakup. Her daddy and my boss are just like that. How do you think my boss would handle me if I hit his best friend's *youngest* son? I'm not dumb."

There are times that try men's souls. Alone. Sulking. Stefan's finger rubbed on the Ping-Pong table's edge, and a sliver went up his nail. Annoyed, he lifted the hand to remove the sliver from his fingernail—when a phantom light turned on over his head.

He saw Carrie as she shifted from one group to go somewhere else. Stefan immediately lifted his hand toward his face and frowned at his finger. Since he could see beyond his hand, he knew when her attention came to him. He worked his mouth subtly as he studied rather dramatically on how to remove the harmless splinter, and he knew as she came toward him.

The fragile splinter almost dropped off, but he shoved it deeper under his nail just in time.

"What's the matter?"

He said with squint-eyed bravery, "It's okay."

She took his hand and got a glimpse of it. "I'll get tweezers. I have some in my purse."

Well. Hell. "Why do you carry them in your purse?"

She lifted her perfect eyebrows and said, "To tweeze my eyebrows."

Stefan asked cautiously, "They grow that fast?"

She gave him a maturely tolerant look. "I'll get the tweezers. Are you all right?"

"Yeah." He looked down, and her face was serious. "I can manage."

She left.

The hero. Hell. Now he'd have to drive it farther under his fingernail so's she could be all sympathetic and struggle to get it out. No one ever knew what all a man went through just to get a little notice from a hard-hearted woman.

He tried to push the fragile bit, and it broke off and fell away! What was left was useless. Well, damn.

He then rapidly peeled back another, more lethal splinter. He hesitated over which finger, then chose the index one instead of the originally involved middle finger. He could handle working without the index finger.

So Stefan stuck the larger splinter up his fingernail—without a shudder, he was so brave. But then Stefan glanced up to see Fred's curious attention.

Fred asked with puzzlement, "What the hell are you doing?"

Stefan replied with warning gentleness, *"Idz do piekla."*

Fred inquired, "You cussing or talking to God."

"I was suggesting you get lost."

"Ohh..." Fred turned to look after Carrie, then he turned back to Stefan with an asinine smile. "You're doing this just to get her attention?"

"If you say one word, I'll do un-re-pair-able harm to your body."

"Yeah?" Fred moved his good body just a tad to call attention to the fact he was not only taller than Stefan but he was bigger. Meaner.

And Stefan replied a deadly, "Yeah."

Fred blinked. "This is serious?"

Through his teeth, Stefan said in a very serious growl, "Get lost."

Fred looked around the Szyszkos' house. "Get lost . . . here?"

Stefan was awesome, "However you can manage—fast enough."

"Well, shhhucks." Then he looked past Stefan to say in a jovial manner, "Your rescuer is here!" And he gave his tolerant killer grin to Carrie.

Naturally, Stefan then turned in such a way that he could jam his finger down against the top of the table and drive the splinter farther up under his nail. The things a man has to do . . . His eyes went out of focus and his lips parted, but he didn't gasp.

Carrie said, "Here," as she reached for his hand. She frowned at his finger. "I misjudged it. This is a bigger splinter than I thought." She looked at him with such sweet concern.

The compassion in her eyes was balm for Stefan's ego. He wasn't aware of the throbbing that went up his arm.

But then Pepper came over and asked in his low voice, "What's the problem?" And whatever it was, Pepper knew he'd straighten it out. That included Stefan Szyszko.

Stefan just gave his ex-friend Pepper a slow look that was deadly.

Carrie said to Pepper, "Move out of the light."

Pepper looked at her as if he hadn't heard right, but the rest of the room began to notice what was going on. There were questions and some replies.

Curious, they moved around the Ping-Pong table, and their concentration was on Stefan and Carrie.

Just about everybody heard as Carrie said to Stefan, "Maybe we ought to take this to Doc Decker?"

But Stefan replied, "No. He's mean, and he'd be rough." Then he looked at her with vulnerable trust. "You do it."

By then the room was just about silent. The women were serious and stretching to see, but the men were awed and absorbing such clever male conduct. A man always tries. He's always watching any man who can find a way to deal with a woman so that he can learn, too. This was important. Getting a woman's sole attention was a real chore. How had Stefan figured out such a tricky way?

Carrie took Stefan into the kitchen, and in the stream of intruding people, she didn't see as Mrs. Szyszko grabbed her husband back from a doorway. They both disappeared.

Stefan saw them, and his heart was pleased. His mother was on his side.

How amazing.

Then he looked at Carrie and tried to figure how the hoyden had won over his *mother?* Carrie could do that? Stefan thought maybe he ought to be a little careful of this obviously fake hell cat.

He allowed her the freedom of his hand. A lost finger would be worth it if he had her attention. Since all the others were crowding around, he didn't squeeze out a single tear.

He saw that she looked at the splinter as if it was a telephone pole. She'd be a softhearted mother... for some man's kids.

She looked up into his face and said, "This'll probably hurt. Want a Popsicle stick to bite on?"

He explained, "We don't have any."

Joe volunteered, "I'll find something."

Pepper said, "I'll help."

The two left the house.

And the rest watched with interest as they waited for Pepper and Joe to return. While they waited, Carrie poured rubbing alcohol into a cup and soaked Stefan's finger.

He inquired with innocence, "Won't the moisture of the alcohol expand the splinter?"

She replied, "Hush. I'm being sterile."

There were too many people around for him to respond to that. The splinter hurt like hell. Or the alcohol did.

Carrie watched his face, then she asked softly, "Want to go to Decker?"

"Nuh-uh."

She pushed his hair back from his forehead and the tip of her finger gently touched his great-grandmother's ring. She said, "You're very brave."

His blue eyes soberly looked at her brown eyes. Quietly brave, he said, "It's a strain."

Just then Joe and Pepper came in with a bite-the-bullet supply of wood. Pepper's contribution was a log. Everyone there hooted or groaned. Pepper just looked at Stefan and was challenging.

Stefan's face was strong and not amused.

However, Joe was more logical. His contribution was a mesquite branch, and everyone knows how hard and mean that wood can be. Joe used his foot to hold the branch while he wrestled a short enough portion without thorns.

The watchers cheered Joe.

He finally had a reasonable section for Stefan. And Stefan said a formal "Thank you," to Joe. He only cast an adult glance at his rival, Pepper.

Joe washed the stick in the sink and soberly offered it to Stefan. Without a snort or laughter from anyone, Stefan took the stick and told Carrie, "I'm ready." Then he put the stick between his teeth.

No one there made any comment at all, but Pepper's face held a larger smile.

Carrie had a hard time, trying to get all the wood out from under Stefan's fingernail. She became so empathetic and upset with the blood that she turned very pale, and her several freckles were apparent.

Around the clenched stick, Stefan watched her, thinking, "You got freckles." He found he'd said it aloud.

She replied, "I do not!" She turned her back to him so that his arm was under hers and his hand was in front of her chest. Now she could see the splinter better and work on it.

Stefan's breathing system went into overdrive.

It was the blood that sundered her. She became wobbly.

"You're lily-livered," Stefan whispered around the mesquite branch between his teeth.

As he knew it would, that comment hit her redheaded temper. She refused to faint. She finished the job. More than likely...there could still be some wood left in all that mess. She released Stefan's arm where it had been clutched against her softness. Then she turned toward him. She frowned up at him and said, "You look fuzzy. You probably ought to sit—" And she fainted.

Stefan had to just about wrestle with Pepper, but he blocked Joe and got to pick up Carrie. He carried her to the living-room sofa and gently put her down. His wound leaked blood all over her pale yellow dress.

Mr. Szyszko came into the living room and said, "What's this? What happened?" He acted unknowing, just as if he hadn't been outside, watching through the kitchen window.

Everybody replied except Stefan. Someone handed Stefan a cool cloth, and he asked for it to be warmed. Carrie was freezing, shivering with nerves. He put an afghan over her with exquisite gentleness. Fainting over a little blood, she'd make a lousy mother for— somebody's kids.

Actually, she'd be compassionate and stridently partial.

Stefan made the rest of the gathered people go into the other room to give Carrie some air.

Minnie the camerawoman said, "She's a wimp." And her eyes steadied on Stefan's face with a slight narrowing of her eyelids.

Stefan knew a woman's friends did that sort of thing to get a commitment from a vulnerable man. He replied kindly, "It's probably the wrong time of the month."

Minnie chided, "You've gotten blood all over her dress and a smear on her face. She needs to be wiped off before she comes to."

He looked at his finger. "Yeah."

Joe came along and offered, "Want it bandaged? I've had first aid. I'm the best bandager in this whole area of TEXAS."

About that time, his mother came with a warm cloth. Without asking any questions, which she would have asked if she'd actually not known why Carrie was out cold on the Szyszkos' sofa, his mother put a warm cloth around her throat. Then she gently wiped Carrie's face and hands with another warm cloth.

Mrs. Szyszko didn't spare one glance to her wounded youngest son. But Joe took Stefan back to the kitchen, washed his hand carefully and bandaged his finger rather elaborately. He advised with logic, "You might as well make the most of it while you can."

Stefan mentioned, "I don't want a sling."

"Well, damn. You just ought not stop a man who's on a roll thisaway. I do a real good sling."

Stefan declined, "No."

Joe suggested, "Keep it tilted up 'til it stops bleeding."

Then somebody said, "She's coming out of it."

Hurrying, Stefan went into the living room and over to the sofa before he actually realized what he was doing. She opened those big brown eyes, and something inside Stefan gasped. His face became very serious.

The two had barely made eye contact when Pepper slid in front of Stefan. Pepper was on his knees beside the prone strawberry-haired treasure. He had very effectively blocked Stefan from Carrie.

Pepper said in a good male voice, "I'll get you out of here."

Carrie reminded Pepper, "Minnie is with me."

"She can follow us."

Carrie was logical. "She can drive me, Pepper. Thanks, anyway." She put a hand to her head, then she asked, "Didn't I just see Stefan? How is his hand?"

Beyond Pepper, Stefan replied, "Mutilated."

Great tears rose in Carrie's eyes. This woman could be brilliantly, painfully, theatrically emotional. She blinked, and everybody soothed her. "You did great!" they said, and, "We think you got it all." And some male voices said, "We can't tell, for sure, through all the blood."

Women scolded, "Hey!" and "Don't say such things to her!" and "Now, shame on you!" "You'll upset her!" "You'll make her cry!"

But the men only laughed.

So Stefan turned on the men and jerked the thumb on his bandaged, injured hand and said, "Out! You're all animals."

That only made them all laugh.

But Carrie saw the elaborate bandage Joe had put on Stefan's hand, and she wailed, "Did I hurt you *that* much?"

Over Joe's ardent protests, Stefan unwound yards of gauze to show her a clean, rather ragged index finger. He said, "It's just this finger." Then he went on earnestly, "You did a real good job on it." The words could mean anything from actual help to mutilation. Men can use words quite cleverly.

On her pale face, Carrie's lipstick was gone and her lips were almost white. She moved them as she said, "We should have taken you to Decker."

Stefan was loyal. "That hatchet man? Never. I prefer you."

That sounded as if Carrie was a kinder, gentler hatchet person. Stefan's index finger was swelling, and it looked terrible.

The men had to mention what it looked like. There were the choices of it being slammed in a door, hit with a tire iron or smashed by a hammer. Things like that. They were quite graphic, and the women exclaimed in protest.

But their talk upset Carrie. That made the guys laugh and tease her about being a cream puff.

She was even more indignant with that accusation.

Stefan told the guys, "Lay off. That's enough!" And he invited them all outside.

They loved it. Pepper went to the door, deadly serious and ready for a good tussle.

Mr. Szyszko came into the room looking so benign that he shut Pepper up, just like that. But Stefan's brothers had stood up. Pepper looked around and saw no one rising for his side, and he had to back down. He did that by saying, "I'll take you home, Carrie."

That declaration only made a couple of real hams begin the Irish song, inserting "again" before her name.

For Minnie, Pat and the rest of the visiting outsiders, it was all a complex, unbalanced night. But for Mac, it brought back long-ago memories of guys ragging each other with such laughter and tussles. He became sentimental and quieter for a while.

For those who were actual Blinkers, it was just another get-together. No Blinker had ever seen a really peaceful gathering. Even in church, the pastor was intrusive. The Blinkers called the attitude being positive, Polish or TEXAN.

It was decided by Carrie, backed by Minnie, that they would see to it that Stefan got home okay. None of the visitors to Stefan's house mentioned the obvious fact that they would be going to the same place. They noted Stefan's narrowed eyes, and they never said one word.

So Stefan's house guests delayed their arrival, and Minnie tactfully stayed in the car as Carrie helped Stefan pull his garage door down, and walked with him into the house. They never locked doors in Blink. Of course, Carrie did, but only in order to shut Stefan out. Otherwise, no one locked their doors.

In the living room, Carrie asked if Stefan would be able to make it up the stairs by himself?

He looked up the ordinary stairway as if looking up at the Matterhorn mountain in the Alps. Bravely, he said a husky, "I think I can." Just like the Little Engine That Could.

So she put her arm around his waist and carefully guided him up the stairs. He glanced down at her face. She was still so pale that he just about felt like a dirty rat to impose on her that way, but he did manage it and even leaned on her, just a tad.

She asked, "Can you undress by yourself?"

And he realized that whole crew of nosy, raucous TV personnel, plus Mac, would be there any minute. What was his guardian angel doing to him? Testing? For crying out loud!

On a hopeless sigh, Stefan said with wobbly bravery, "I'll be okay."

"If I loosen your belt and undo the buttons, can you do the rest?"

With faint uncertainty, he replied, "Yes."

"Oh, Stefan. I should have insisted you go to Dr. Decker."

Stefan repeated, "He's a butcher."

Carrie said sadly, "I didn't do much better."

His voice was gentle and earnest. He seemed so honest as he reassured her. "You were brilliant. You're like an angel of mercy." His voice clacked with his earnestness. But his ears heard a car try to get in the driveway. It was blocked by Minnie, who was waiting for Carrie.

Stefan did what he had to do, he gave Carrie a killer kiss. It was gentle, tender and insinuating. It was a brain wobbler for a susceptible woman. She was sweet.

When she could, she pushed back from him. She mumbled, "Good night. I hope you can sleep okay." She turned away.

Softly, he reminded her, "My belt and buttons." While she apparently didn't notice, Stefan could hear the conversation and laughter out in his driveway, so apparently Minnie was still keeping the horde at bay. He could not lose this chance to have Carrie almost undress him.

Her fingers fumbled. She was still recovering from his kiss. She undid his shirt and unbuckled his trousers. Then she looked up into his face blindly and said, "Your breathing isn't good. Are you all right?"

She wasn't even focusing her eyes. He said softly, "Thank you, Carrie. You're so sweet."

Just to show how off balance she was, she nodded in a floppy manner and started to open the door to the closet.

Gently, he took her arm and led her to the actual door. He guided her through it, and faced the fact that she'd have to manipulate the stairs. And he knew she needed him to get her down them.

So he led her down the wicked, tricky steps and to the front door. Again she nodded in a wobbly manner, went through the door and had to stop to sort out which car was hers.

Minnie got out and came to her. She looked past Carrie to Stefan in the slitted front door with his clothes unbuttoned and his shirttails out.

Minnie blinked a time or two, then she led the zombie who was Carrie over to her own car. Minnie waved the others aside and waited as they backed their cars out onto the road. And with the way clear, the two women left.

Four

———

Quickly, before the horde erupted into his house, Stefan closed the front door. He then adroitly put his clothing together, buttoned and zipped. A man can do all sorts of things without an index finger. That's why he'd chosen that one for the splinter, instead of the more vulnerable middle finger.

While he hurriedly tidied himself, he peripherally faced the possibility of infection. The deliberately impaled splinter was a deep penetration and the removal had been done by a very sweet amateur. He looked at the bloodied mess and considered the projected consequences. It was a vulnerable injury and infection really was a possibility.

Infection? *Great!* He'd have her sympathy. Her guilt. Her attention. The damned finger hurt like hell. She'd be appalled and she'd blame herself. Stefan smiled like a cream-fed cat. Then he sighed. Women were such a nuisance. The things a man had to do to get attention would boggle any ordinary woman.

But she'd be racked by guilt! A man just took advantage of a woman's guilt. He'd become bedridden as the infection spread and she'd volunteer to sit with him and put cool cloths on his fever-hot head. Then maybe he'd chill and she'd have to strip and climb into bed with him to warm him. *Yes!*

Stefan considered the whole situation, and gradually he understood he was sitting in the catbird seat. All he had to do was reel her in.

Uhh... She wasn't the type for an affair. As he climbed the stairs to his portion of his crowded room, he considered that she'd already underlined her rejection of an affair. She'd dumped him. She wanted permanence. Well, first he needed to look around at other women.

He would. He would. No man should pull the trap of marriage over his head until he was ready to quit looking around.

However, in the meanwhile, he could milk Carrie's sympathy and her guilt for mutilating his index finger. He'd just see how he did with her.

But he'd have to go slow. She was chancy, and he would have to see how far he could push her guilt.

With the filming crew there at his place, Stefan was hampered for privacy. But, with them there, Carrie did come over. She felt perfectly safe with him since she always had Minnie along. And Minnie had to be along since she was the cameraperson.

As the people-crowded days passed, Stefan watched bitterly as his finger healed. No infection. No crippling. No problem. A lost opportunity. Another one gone down the drain.

He would have been disgruntled, but each time Carrie saw him she reached for his hand and examined it carefully. She would be sympathetic and ask him how it was.

He was brave and very quiet.

That way, Stefan got to stand close to her and look at her while she examined his hand. His breaths were shallow and uneven. His libido was stimulated. God, was he stimulated!

Then she would look up at him with those brown eyes of hers and say, "It's better. Maybe I didn't cripple you for life."

If she only knew! But he replied gallantly, "You saved my finger." And he added earnestly, "Decker would have amputated it."

With that, her eyes sparkled and her lips smiled at him, just about ruining him for normal speech.

Carrie's boss at the local TV station felt he was too old to go running around the countryside with a bunch of wet-eared kids, so he let Carrie do the local color. She had taped Mac's remembrances of how it was in the South Pacific in World War II. A war in something called the *Pacific?* How could that be?

Pacific meant peaceful. The ocean should be renamed . . . Turmoil.

Starting with Mac, something about the outsiders was on the TV every single night. Not Carrie, more's the pity, but the local people and what they were doing to get involved with the professional shoot of Mac and the hotshot World War II pilot.

The pilot's name was Jerold Kraut. Of course, Kraut for a last name was bad enough, but he was called Jerry. Since the enemy in World War I were called Jerrys, Kraut found that droll.

He was little and cocky and humorous. Mac allowed him to share his room. However, since Jerry had been only a shavetail second lieutenant, he slept on a cot in Mac's room at Stefan's house. Mac had the double bed to himself.

Jerry was a laugh. He strutted and teased. He was one hell of a pilot. He could fly any of the small planes. He'd never flown the big bombers, he'd been a fighter pilot. But any of the little planes were playthings. He was scarily brilliant as a pilot.

Every year, he went to the fly-in reunions of the pilots. So barnstorming around Blink was no big deal for him. He was in his element.

Mac treated Jerry with stern, adult tolerance, just exactly the way any World War II master sergeant had treated any shavetail. Their current ages had no softening effect on Mac's conduct.

It had been a long, long time since Jerry had dealt with someone like Mac, and Jerry was amused. Ole Mac was now too old to deal with the reparations Jerry had doled out to other snide, scoffing sergeants of fifty years ago. So the only response to Mac was Jerry's amusement dancing in his eyes. That and an occasionally bitten lip when his humor almost got out of hand.

There were several men in Blink who were veteran flyers of the Second World War. They loved the meetings at the Szyszkos' house. There was the talk and remembering. They'd rarely speak of the bad things or the serious, scary things. Their talk was of the mistakes and solving them. The absolutely hilarious things they pulled on other pilots and the responses. Most of which, in the telling, had gradually been altered just a tad.

Pat was smart enough to tape and film such.

Then Jerry's wife, Donna, drove into town in a convertible. That woman, who refused to fly, was driving like a bat out of hell.

The senior Szyszkos' took her in, and Jerry moved out of Mac's room at Stefan's and joined his wife at the Szyszkos' house. He explained to Mac, "She's a quieter sleeper than you."

So Mac again had the room at Stefan's all to himself, and he missed Jerry's company. He missed the sharing.

Stefan listened to all the chatter and felt left out. There were a lot of guys in Blink, plus those who were involved in the shoot, who'd been in Vietnam. There were even five Blinkers who'd been in Desert Storm. All those available from all the wars crowded into the senior Szyszkos' house, and they told stories. They laughed and competed and shared. They bonded.

Stefan considered his normal life and didn't cherish it. His years had fallen between conflicts. He felt he'd had no adventure at all.

He didn't consider all the horrible times the men weren't talking about. They rarely mentioned those. They couldn't afford to spend the emotion it would take to remember and relive it. So they rarely told of the terror, the discomfort in living and waiting.

Stefan didn't understand about the debit side. He listened to their sharing. Then he looked at his own life and found it wanting, unshared with other men in danger. His life was too safe. It was lacking.

So. Was the US of A supposed to get into another tangle just to allow Stefan Szyszko an adventure? And he *considered* it!

Bosnia did cool a human's interest in war. Territory disputes and ethnic cleansing. What a terrible mess. Would there ever be stories around a Yugoslavian fire that made others laugh? How could there be? And yet . . . and yet, World War II had been no different. It, too, had been about territorial greed, power and ethnic cleansing. The only difference was the territorial greed had been worldwide.

With all the older men sitting on the chairs in his parents' house, Stefan sat on the floor with his back against the wall, and he listened. He laughed. He sat up late with all the rest as the older men told their stories.

It had been just so since caveman days. Not much progress. The only difference was in weapons.

The weather delayed the shoot. Since the Szyszkos were so generous in their hospitality, they did need to get Stefan's car lot in the background. By then, Mac's old Jeep was tilted up on a slowly rotating pole out in front of the building. The suspended Jeep could be seen from some distance. It was a surprise for those strangers who happened by.

Jerry's visitors didn't complain about the sundered Jeep, it was Mac's cohorts. The pilots weren't particularly Jeep-oriented. It was the old soldiers who were shocked to see a good Jeep impaled on a pole. They mentioned to each other that it was like it'd happened to them, personally.

While the ground and air veterans gave lip service to each other's need in the war, they gradually drifted apart. Mac held court in the family room, while the pilots kept to the kitchen.

It was the women coming into the gatherings and giving their own stories that boggled the men from the earlier wars. Those women from the Vietnam war spoke of those still on active duty after Desert Storm. There were even women *pilots* in Desert Storm. Men's bastions were crumbling.

Crumbling?

From the beginning of time, women had been involved in all the wars. Actively involved. Fighting. The only difference was muscle strength ... and being vulnerable. They had never been sheltered. In all the wars in all time, the women were there and they had participated.

Like the men, the women didn't speak of the horrors, but their stories were ironically droll. "I climbed down from the plane, and he swatted my butt with exuberance. He was laughing and saying unmentionable things. When I took off my helmet, he said, 'Uhh...' Then he looked at my hands. He turned white and couldn't think of a thing more to say. So I told him it really *was* what he'd said. But he was still frozen in shock."

Stefan listened. And at night he dreamed of being a hero ... to Carrie. He would waken in his torn-up bed and lie there ... disgruntled. Claiming only a splinter fragment under his fingernail, how could he be a hero?

Again Pat and his crew were somewhere else, working at other projects as they waited for Blink's weather to be perfect. TEXAS weather is always perfect, it's just differently "perfect" at various times.

When Pat left, so did his camerawoman. So Stefan didn't have quite as much contact with Carrie in those times. But she still came over when Mac was there, and she would include Stefan in her conversation.

She still wasn't an anchorwoman on the local TV. Stefan was holding his breath over that. She might apply somewhere else. She might leave Blink before he could...before... And Stefan sobered and considered before what?

What were his plans for Carrie?

Nothing.

Nothing?

Well... He just wanted her around while he decided if he did want some plans for her. He really ought to quit thinking so much about Carrie until he'd looked around at other women.

During the periods of Pat's absence from Blink, life did go on. Jerry and his wild woman went home, but Mac comfortably continued to stay in the room at Stefan's place. He didn't go on home.

Stefan didn't mind at that time, because he didn't want to fool around with any women he'd brought home. With some of the drop-by women, Mac was a chaperon and a good deterrent. Stefan couldn't not be amused by that. After all, he was thirty! He didn't need a chaperon.

But there was a time or two when he was glad old Mac horned in on the conversation with a female drop-by. There were women who were shockingly aggressive! It was not a surprise, but Stefan felt some shock and watched Mac's tact in coping as chaperon.

One day Carrie met Stefan downtown and stopped as he said a smiling greeting. He didn't realize he always smiled when he saw her.

Carrie said snippily, "I understand Petey Lou came by to see you yesterday?" It was the questioning statement.

He shook his head slowly, his mind going over the people at the car lot. Then he remembered Petey had come by his house. He said, "Oh. She came to see Mac."

"Why...Mac?"

"I don't know. I wasn't downstairs."

So Mac was a mixed blessing. The problem was that the old man was so much "to home" in Stefan's house. Mac met the older neighborhood men and before Stefan could blink, it wasn't even two weeks, for crying out loud, that the old man had organized a pinochle group. That wasn't so bad, but they met at Stefan's house and used his kitchen table.

Just about every night, Mac would greet the returning Stefan and add, "We're about out of beer."

Stefan bought the kind that had no alcohol. The kind for hunters and boaters. The old men couldn't read the fine print, and they were contented with the taste.

One of the good things about Mac was that he didn't ride horses. Most of the pinochle bunch didn't ride, but on occasion there would be a substitute whose horse-dander residue really made Stefan's eyes water.

On one occasion Carrie's father and Stefan's father came by to see Mac during the day. The group added another table.

And during the games, the fathers of Stefan and Carrie mentioned the stymied attraction that pulled their offspring, male and female. Mac rubbed his grizzled, unshaven face and nodded.

After that, when women casually dropped by Stefan's house, Mac was the greeter... and he was a visitor. But if Carrie had some reason to stop off at Stefan's, Mac disappeared from sight. He was still in the house, but he'd moved up to his room, turned on the TV and was silent.

For Stefan, having Mac around was as bad as living at home.

But how could Stefan get rid of such an entrenched guest before the shoot was accomplished? If Mac wasn't there, would Carrie still come by?

Stefan mentioned to his father that it would be nice if Mac moved in with him and his mother because then they could all play pinochle.

Mr. Szyszko replied reasonably, "One car wouldn't carry all the player-neighbors around you. Not very many of those older people can drive. I'm not yet retired, and I'm not a chauffeur."

That was plain enough, and Stefan accepted that he had a guest who was his responsibility. He wouldn't be able to palm him off onto some other host.

It was a very interesting thing for Carrie to witness the kind tolerance Stefan gave to his intrusive, tenacious takeover guest. However, Mac being in Stefan's house was all that allowed Carrie excuses to be quite bold in finding reasons for visiting the young bachelor.

She always had good reason for being there. It was something to do with the shoot, not yet accomplished, or the town meeting, or his opinion on how to handle some odd project assigned to her.

Stefan took it all seriously and gave her careful advice. Her questioning was so structured that he wasn't entirely sure she was concocting reasons to see him. She was probably just legitimately asking for advice. While that was flattering, he really wanted her pining for him.

He touched her. He looked forward to the times that he could put a casual-seeming hand on her arm or at her waist. Her damned short hair didn't need his fingers to take the strands from her mouth or smooth them behind her ear.

She was a real nuisance to his libido. She didn't fall against him and rub her different body against his needy one and swoon with her sexual need of him. She was pert and businesslike, and her questioning always seemed to be germane.

It flattered him to have her look at him with those big brown eyes of hers and listen to what he said. He'd never before considered that he was a man whom people needed. With four raucous, pushy big brothers, he'd never before been consulted about *any*thing.

Now, Carrie needed him. She sought his opinions about the town, and sometimes she threw him with the presence of a problem he hadn't known existed in Blink. And he had the maturity to say so and add, "I'll check it out."

With the drop-ins at his car lot, he got a lot of information, but he went beyond that and asked the people involved for input. He was then consulted in town because he appeared to be so well informed. By then, he was.

It occurred to him that Carrie could have well done that very same thing. She didn't need him or his research.

She was using him? No, she was using that ruse to be around him, so that he could feel she needed him. It was a heady knowledge. And he waited to see what she'd try next.

She hadn't been able to get an interview with an old lady in a nursing home. The woman refused. She'd had a very tough life in early Blink, and she was very old. Carrie asked Stefan, "How can I get an interview? What angle could I use? Right now, she declines even seeing me."

And as if it was logical, Stefan said, "Take Mac with you."

Carrie scoffed. "He's young enough to be her son."

That surprised Stefan. "Is he?" So she must never have noticed how Mac talked to women?

Then Carrie thoughtfully asked Stefan, "How can I approach Mac on this?"

"Tell him he would be an interesting guest for a solitary woman. He's sly and he's a flirt. But even more important than that, he's not needed anymore."

Carrie heard the last words and nodded gently. Then she asked Stefan, "How would she know about him?"

"Make an appointment with her so that she can be primped up. Don't just walk in on her. She might want a pretty bed jacket. See if she has one."

And it worked. Mac was gentle and smooth. He was very alive and masculine in that environment. In her pretty bed jacket with her hair in an elegant swirl, the lady was charmed. The interview was gentle, and the portion on TV was kind. Carrie gave all credit to Stefan and to Mac.

It seemed that everyone in Blink saw the interview. The Home called the station and said several people remembered the lady and put themselves on the list as visitors for her.

With that information, Carrie had another excuse to drop by to see Stefan. "There is a big change in the lady. She is more alert. She's enjoying the visits."

"Good."

"I am so grateful for your advice. You're always right."

Very seriously, he said, "I have a problem you can solve." He said that knowing full well that Mac was upstairs.

Carrie was equally serious. "What is your problem?" Her voice was hesitant.

"I need to kiss you."

She watched him for a while before she replied, "Oh." Then she said, "I don't think it's wise. You tend to get very hyper."

And he opened out his arms and his face was benign as he dredged up that old saw, "I'm older. I have control now."

What idiot woman would fall for any such bushwah? Carrie did.

She moved just a hesitant tad toward him, and he took over. His arms wrapped around her like boa constrictors, as he pulled her tightly against him and he kissed her. It was stunning.

When he lifted his mouth in order to judge his victim, she said "That was pleasant," and she released herself from him and went out through the kitchen door. She hesitated at the back screen door and turned around to see the pirate who was Stefan standing in the kitchen doorway, watching what she would do.

She smiled kindly and said, "Goodbye." She went out the back screen door and down the steps. There she looked around before she looked down the driveway to where her car was parked in the front yard. She trudged toward it valiantly, as if against a strong wind.

Stefan's hot eyes glittered. He had to put his hands into his pants pockets and push down until his arms were straight. He had to breathe out through pursed lips. He had to walk around and lean his head back. But he at least knew which was the front door and which was the back door.

After Carrie had allowed Stefan to tease her into kissing her, they began to date again. She was cautious. He was selling. She declined to give up the other two men she was dating. Pepper was one.

Sitting with her in his car in a secluded woody place, Stefan declared, "Nobody goes with more than one man at a time."

She replied, "Only smart women. No smart woman commits to dating one man until she's sure."

He was offended. "You are testing me?"

"Yes."

"Well, what's good for the goose is good for the gander."

She watched very seriously.

He said no more.

But he let go of all the stops when he took her home and kissed her good night.

After that he began kissing her during the evening. Any excuse gave him the idea. It was Monday. There was a shooting star....

"Where?" She looked around out of the car's windows, searching for such an amazing thing.

"It just shot across the sky. Didn't you see it?"

"No," she replied, still looking. "Which way?"

"I saw it. I get a kiss."

"You've had your share for today."

"You're a pain..." he began with some irritation. Then he brightened and asked with interest, "Would you like to know where?"

"Behave." She settled back into her side of the front seat.

Disgruntled, he replied, "You ask the impossible."

She gestured and was reasonable. "You're civilized and—"

"Who told you that?" And his tone was offended.

Explaining logically, she instructed, "This is a period of sorting out our feelings—"

"You want feelings?"

"Cut that out!" she scolded. "This is a time of seeing if we rub well together."

"Let's see." He lifted her against him with her wiggling.

She exclaimed, "No! Not now. Stop it! *Stefan,* quit that!"

"You *said* we rub well together. I was just seeing if we did."

"I meant we're fairly companionable. You—"

"I like the rubbing part."

"I believe you're a sex fiend."

"Yeah." Nodding in considering, head-bouncing agreement, he continued his helpful openness, "Probably."

"What *else* are you in a relationship? Can you cope if I'm ill or if the kids are sick? Could you—"

"Sure."

"How do you know?"

"I want an affair. I need to have one before I settle down and behave—publicly. I want to see if you're a willing partner or if you only endure. I need to test your responses. A man's a fool to walk into a marriage without knowing what he's getting into."

"Then you agree that we must get to know and understand each other...first."

"Yeah. Come here, woman, and let's get acquainted." He pushed back the seat on his side and said, "Slide over the console and come on over here."

She sighed and clasped her hands on her lap and looked out of her window into the darkness. "We're back to where we were when we broke up."

"Why didn't you object sooner?"

"I did. You weren't listening. Look, Stefan, this is a mistake. Just take me on home."

He was indignant. "Why?"

"We aren't suited."

"If we weren't, you wouldn't be bending my brain the way you do." He was getting terse and somewhat impatient. "What sort of marriage do you want? A careful, structured, scheduled relationship? Three Saturdays a month?"

"Take me home."

He refused. "No. This is what split us up the last time. I need to know if you're a cold woman who just wants a meal ticket and two and one-third children."

Rather sadly, she said, "I think it's down to one and a half, now."

"Well, the half one shouldn't be too difficult to birth." His tone was sour.

Carrie was rather tense as she said, "Obviously, we can't talk. You might just as well take me home."

Stefan told her, "We aren't on the same wavelength. It's you who can't talk. You just want to sit over there primly and in control, when I'm going out of my mind from wanting you."

"Testosterone."

In a drivingly steady voice, he replied, "There's nothing wrong with being male. I don't complain because you're female, all tight and prissy and—right!"

She tilted her head as if listening. "That sounds suspiciously like a complaint!"

"Yeah. You're right. I've been trying for you for so long I've forgotten why I really want you. I love you, you holdout."

But she didn't melt and spread herself over him. She said tight-lipped, "You have marvelous ways of showing it."

His voice got reedy, "I can show you a better way."

"That's all you think about!"

"Don't you?" he asked with earnestness. "How can you kiss me that way and not feel any...want?"

She looked at him and her eyes were enormous. "Of course I do."

He was silent for a minute, then his voice hoarse, he asked gently, vulnerably, "You do?"

"I have control."

"Well, hell." He lifted his arms and dropped them. But he asked softly, "How steely is your control?"

She looked over at him and tilted her head back. "Like iron."

He quickly drew a deeply irritated breath of disgust and exhaled immediately. "Yeah. I'll vouch for that."

He levered his seat forward in a jerk and started the car.

They didn't speak again all the way to her house. As they turned into her street, he asked, "You still dating Pepper?"

"Of course."

"You're not being fair to him."

"Why do you say that?"

"You know good and well that it's me you love, and eventually we'll get married. You'll leave him hanging. It isn't kind."

She explained so that he wouldn't worry about it, "I've promised him to somebody else."

He rolled the car silently into her driveway and turned off the engine. He turned his head and looked at her. Then he repeated her words, "You've—promised—him to somebody—else?"

Carrie gathered her sweater and purse as she told him logically, "She'll make him a good wife. She wants him. She's betting you'll get me. I'm not as sure."

Stefan couldn't let it go. "But you are arranging Pepper's life, now, in case you turn him down?"

"Of course."

Stefan lay his forearm over his steering wheel and contemplated the night with serious thought. Then he turned his head and looked at the silent woman, back at home and still sitting in his car.

She hadn't popped out and run into the house. She was waiting for... what? So he said again, "If you're serious about me, then you ought to leave Pepper be. You could really hurt him."

With lifted eyebrows, she enunciated, "I am very surprised you are so compassionate for Pepper. You are enemies."

"Not until you got out of college and came home. We were friends before then."

"You were friends?" she asked, surprised.

"Just like Jeff and Joe and the others."

So she questioned, "Then why don't you let me go?"

"I did!" he replied in irritation. "And you started coming around and calling my attention to yourself. Asking me all sorts of questions and badgering me for— Hold on, there, I haven't finished!"

In a deadly voice, she promised, "I'll leave you alone! You beast! Pepper is a gentleman . . . compared to you!"

"What do you mean, 'compared' to me? What's he done?"

She snapped, "It's none of your business. Let me go before I holler for my daddy."

In disgust, releasing her, he snarled, "You'd do that, too!"

" 'Too!' I haven't done anything, yet! Let go!"

"I took you out and you owe me a good-night kiss, and I'm not leaving 'til I get one." He pulled her against him and kissed her exactly as he wanted.

Did she really allow him to drag her back against him? Did she help? He wasn't at all sure, but she did put her hand up to his face and gently touched his cheek in a very brief almost-touch before she wiggled and pushed at him.

He lifted his mouth from hers, still holding her resisting body, and he said to that useless woman, "You kissed me back."

"I did not!"

Five

————

Carrie pried herself loose from Stefan and moved back to her side of his car. She'd opened her door and was out of his car before he could stop her. She had zipped up the steps to her porch before he reached the bottom stop. He growled to her in a voice accurately set to reach only her ears, "Wait."

She glanced dismissively over her shoulder, back at Stefan. She did not wait but just went on to the door. She had it open before he could get there. So she was inside with the screen door hooked by the time he was at the door.

How like a woman to be so unkind.

With his voice softened to resemble a whisper, Stefan said through his teeth, "You didn't thank me for a lovely evening."

She responded politely in a whisper, "Most of it was nice." Then her big brown eyes looked at him patiently.

"Nice?" His response was a little stronger sound.

She was adjustable. "Pleasant."

"I give up." He turned and started back off the porch, toward his car.

In a perfectly normal, soft voice she said, "Good night."

He paused and turned back as he asked quite seriously, "What was good about it?"

However, Carrie had closed the front door and there was no reply.

He stood there on the porch, listening, but he could hear no indication that she moved inside the house. And she didn't open the door and come back outside.

He gave up. He sighed deeply, with his mouth closed, and went back to his car. He got in and waited, in case she'd come out to the porch railing. She did not. He started the car and slowly backed away, watching the house. She didn't come back out to wave to him.

Fortunately, his trained reflexes caused him to glance up at the rearview mirror in time to slam on the brakes. Since he'd been creeping along, he didn't run into Pepper's car... sitting between the cement pillars, on the apron of the drive with the headlights off, blocking Stefan's egress.

So. Here was The Confrontation? With great endurance, Stefan turned off the motor and set the brake. He got out of the car and walked with practiced, casual, loose, dangerous slowness toward Pepper's car.

The slow walk was copied from Stefan's big brothers. It was rather elaborately paced, with slouched body language that said for Pepper to be smart and run along home or he was in trouble.

Stefan had the mind flashback to being sixteen years old again, and he found the relationship droll. Surely Pepper was old enough to be reasonable? He, too, was thirty.

Pepper opened the door of his car.

Now, what the hell was Stefan to do? He'd just given the lecture to Carrie about not harming Pepper, and now *he* was supposed to hit him? Pepper had to be smarter than to trigger that juvenile behavior. They were men now, on the very Brink to begin to take over the running of Blink. Right? Big deal.

Within a hushed distance, Stefan said to Pepper, "Just go on home and leave this be."

"You already dumped her."

Stefan deliberately slowed his words so that Pepper couldn't consider them argumentative. He replied, "No. I was giving her thinking room."

"You could hurt her." Pepper's voice was stern. "Leave her be."

"Pepper, you're my friend. You need to know I'm serious about this budding woman who needs a little struggle so as she'll feel she won when I give in. You know that. She belongs to me."

The contender shook his head. "That's not the signals I get."

Stefan's reply was adult and reasonable, "I hate to tell you this, Pepper, but she's using you to test me."

"I don't see it thataway." Pepper slowly shook his head. "You back off and let her decide. I'm not giving up."

To show how confident he was, Stefan put his hands into his pant pockets and sighed hugely as he looked around, but he peripherally kept Pepper in sight...and was ready to avoid being attacked.

Women were a nuisance.

Stefan said, "I feel like I'm sixteen again and dating...what was her name? Margie?"

"Mary Lou."

"Yeah." Stefan remembered with some nostalgia. Sixteen was a long time ago.

"Remember Audrey?"

Stefan leaned against Pepper's fender. "Man alive, she really stirred a guy up. But she just did it to see if she could."

Pepper leaned against his car door and observed, "Women are strange."

Stefan gestured one slow hand to indicate the futility of it all. "We don't have any other choice."

"Yeah. I want Carrie."

Very easily kind, Stefan said, "Naw. You don't really. You're just competitive."

"No."

Stefan smiled and scoffed. "You've been competitive with me ever since I got that basket from across the line as the whistle blew."

"What a throw." Pepper shook his head once as he studied the ground in front of him.

"Luck." Stefan labeled it with adult ease. "Blind luck. Everybody gets one 'shot' of some kind that works, and that was mine." Then he added reflectively, "Given the choice, I think I'd have chosen something else besides an impossible basketball shot."

At Carrie's house—which belonged to her parents but was labeled as hers—the door opened and a male figure came out onto the porch.

Since Stefan was looking that way, he saw her brother Sean first.

Pepper had to turn his head to look. "What's Sean doing home?"

"He probably needs money and came home to bond a bit before asking."

"You do that, too?"

"It's in the freshman-orientation book."

"I never read mine. I should have. I probably missed basics."

Sean had walked soundlessly across the porch, down the steps and came indolently along the drive to where the two driveway blockers were visiting.

They were silent as Sean approached. Then Stefan asked, "Come to referee?"

"You all going to tussle over that fluff? Why don't you just draw straws? You got my momma concerned. She woke me out of the best hot dream I've ever had in my life, and I'm feeling a little hostile."

"I've had dreams like that," Stefan was sympathetic.

Pepper groused, "Mine are always interrupted by Stefan, who horns in."

Stefan was amazed and exclaimed, "You have that kind, too?"

Sean said, "Go home. I'm here only for the weekend. I don't have time to come out here and argue with two yahoos who are snarling over the same bone who is my sister."

"We was just visitin'." Stefan was tolerant.

"You got all the neighbors out of their beds, and their noses are pressed to the windows. People have grease on their skins and the windows are getting smudged. As good citizens in favor of unsmudged windows . . . leave this place, now."

Stefan said to Pepper, "He's six years younger than us. What right has he got to order his elders around?"

Pepper replied thoughtfully, "We gonna teach him manners?"

Sean's breath picked up—

Stefan said in a remembering way, "Remember when Lyle got all hot and bothered about—uh—the redhead . . . carroty red."

Sean's voice squeaked, "Lucy?"

Pepper exclaimed, "Now how'd you remember her?"

Sean shrugged, "She had that red hair and she'd gotten those big lumps on her chest that jiggled, and we were . . . fascinated." He lighted a cigarette and drew the smoke deep into his lungs.

Stefan commented thoughtfully, "Yeah. She was eye-catching, all right. The guy she married took her off somewheres else."

Pepper added, "She's got six kids now."

And the other two gasped.

Stefan asked, "How'd you hear about that?"

But just then Mr. Rodway, from across the street, strolled over and exchanged greetings. Then he asked, "Car trouble?"

It was predictably Stefan the soother who replied, "Naw. Just talking."

"You got my woman curious," Mr. R chided.

Stefan suggested, "Give her a wave, and then tell us about what sort of unmarried women our mommas were."

Mr. R did turn and give one big wave toward his house; then he turned back and told Sean, "Put out that dirty, old cigarette. You're too young to smoke."

Showing the kind of man he was by then, Sean made no comment and did as directed.

Mr. R leaned a hip on Pepper's back fender and began, "Stefan, your momma was the biggest trial we ever had in this whole, entire county. We would have *paid* your papa to've carried her off. There was fights all over the place with men trying to usurp one another in contention for her. We'd all shake our heads over that bitty. Your daddy was the only man to control her."

"My sweet mamma?"

Mr. Rodway was surprised. "Didn't you know?"

"Nobody ever told me!"

Mr. R told the rest of it, "You've heard of a woman being a handful? She was two hands full."

"What about mine?" Pepper asked. His mother had divorced his father, left Pepper with him and taken off.

In a moony way, Mr. R replied, "She was a love. She really admired you. She was so kind and gentle, but she did have an independent streak, you see, and—"

Sam Pierce came along. "Is this a meeting to decide on the new mayor?"

Since he *was* the mayor, his neighbor, Mr. R, replied, "Yeah. Got any suggestions? The man we now have is... Oh, is that you, Mayor Pierce?"

After the prerequisite chuckle, the mayor asked, "What's the discussion?"

And Stefan replied, "Recalcitrant women."

"Oh," said the mayor. "If this is such a serious discussion, we ought to go down to Joe's Bar and really look at the issue."

Stefan declined. He shook his head and said, "After tussling with your dau— That was *verbal* tussling, you understand? I just have to get myself home before I drop from exhaustion. She is an arguer. She get that from her politician papa?"

The mayor shook his head. "I'm a peaceable man. I can see and weigh both sides. That's why I was chosen as the balanced head of this vital office in Blink. It's her mama. You name the subject, and she'll take either side."

Stefan was aghast! He exclaimed, "I hope this information is in time! Did you hear that, Pepper?"

"I like contentious women. Back off."

"Oh, *ho,* we've got a real balance here. As mayor of this fair c—"

"Papa, they're fighting over Carrie. They are not balanced."

"Are you interrupting?" Carrie and Sean's own father reared back his head.

"When I get out of law school, I'm going to be county prosecutor?" The do-you-understand questioning statement.

"Lord, save us all," their neighbor, Mr. Rodway, exclaimed. "The Pierce family will be just like the Fergusons."

Slowly, thoughtfully shaking his head, the mayor replied, "I don't think we're that dramatic."

So they all discussed politics, personalities, the beef market and some odds and ends. Nothing was solved.

Inside the Pierce house, halfway down the stairs, the Pierce mother and daughter were sitting, watching out the glass fan over the front door. The men moved around and shifted and obviously they all talked and gestured.

Carrie asked, "What are they saying?"

"Bonding things. They probably haven't even mentioned you and Stefan and Pepper. They're talking baseball or football or politics or fishing or dove hunting or something similar. Men are very strange creatures." She looked at her only daughter and gave her sage advice. "They are the only choice we have. They are all of them variations of your father and brother."

"Good gravy."

"There are the perks," her mother offered some comfort.

Carrie slid doubting eyes over to her mother and asked, "Like?"

"Besides sex, they're mostly loyal, supportive and they share. They share colds, debts and vast varieties of problems. They are endlessly fascinating. Look at them. They're all out there soothing two high testosterone-plagued men, whose drive right now is finding a woman of their own.

"If it wasn't for that drive, men would run around exhausting themselves doing all sorts of things like space travel, hunting deer, digging canals and God only knows what all, but it would be highly competitive and they'd never let up. We give them some respite from themselves."

Carrie sighed. "Life isn't easy."

"If it was, it would be boring. Look at the physical turmoil on this earth. The floods and storms, the earthquakes and solar eclipses ... and our wonderful curiosity. How boring it would be without it all. That, and the opposing thumb that makes us able to solve things and build."

Carrie observed, "You've always been interesting. Who else would use this meeting of five men, down on our driveway, to give a lecture on the wonders of this world?"

Her mother slid a look at her child and grinned.

Carrie said bravely, "I'm not mad at Stefan." The silence inside the house lengthened. Carrie added, "I would like to yell at him."

"I know."

"His thumb is short and stubby. You've said that's the sign of a stubborn man."

"Determined," her mother mused.

After another pause, Carrie mentioned, "His palm does have the *M* that is the old soul."

"That would invite consideration."

Thoughtfully, Carrie mused, "His lifeline curls around the base of his thumb. He'll live forever."

"That's nice."

"Mother, you're being irritatingly neutral."

"It's past the time that I can influence you."

"How cowardly."

But her mother only laughed, so softly, so intimately sharing, that Carrie had to smile, but she shook her head.

The fivesome on the apron of the Pierce driveway were visiting for almost two hours before the mayor stretched and mentioned the time. They agreed to go rabbit hunting two days later, and they parted.

Pepper went to his car and backed onto the street and turned the car away, but he only inched along until he saw Stefan back from the Pierce driveway and go on off, too.

As Stefan drove home, he remembered that he needed to look at other women. He kept forgetting that. But he needed something to distract Pepper from Carrie. Hmm. Yeah. And when he got home, very carefully and with great skill, he removed a loose brick in the fireplace and took out his little black book.

He'd hidden it there the first time Carrie had come to his house. He knew full well that, with her there, he'd get a phone call to go to the car lot, and she'd be alone in the house. Women did that. Then they cleverly went through *everything* very carefully, leaving no trace but knowing every one of a man's secrets.

He'd be gone and his house would be vulnerable, with no protective host. She'd find the black book... first.

Then she'd copy down all the names and phone numbers, and she'd call and meet all those names for lunch. She'd probe and cross-examine and dig. She would.

She'd do that while she still lived at home with her mama and papa, at her age, and she would snoop in his house.

However, while she had been at his place, there had been no phone call. But the anticipation of one, and listening for it, had ruined his evening. He hadn't had the nerve to attempt a seduction.

He hadn't even gotten hot with her. Her parents had known where she was. She'd mentioned them when she'd brought in the cake she said she'd made.

There were good things about a little town, but the negatives were overwhelming for a courting man, an itchy man, a needy man.

In male-bonding meetings, Stefan would slide his eyes around, trying to find a nontalking man who could give him some suggestions on how to get Carrie off somewhere else just with him. There must be some way a man could get a woman alone for long enough.

There was no such help. And how could he ask Pepper where he'd taken that temporary woman on a weekend? Pepper would want to know which woman Stefan had in mind, or he would have shown up at the place wanting to switch women. No way.

Women were a pain.... Yeah. And Stefan moved his body in sensual agony.

Having considered the matter seriously, Stefan came to the conclusion that the thing to do was to find Pepper another woman.

So, of course, he went through the little black book with fond nostalgia. All of the women listed were more pliant and easier to be around than Carrie.

If that was true, then why had he let all those women get away? He'd been too young. Naw. That hadn't been the problem. The truth of the matter was that none of them had been Carrie.

He was really hooked?

Then why did he feel this reluctance?

He walked around his house, holding the treasured black book with its precious listings in his hand, unnoticed. His problem was that he wanted Carrie to want him as much as he wanted her. He needed to test her, to see if she could be distracted from him.

Surely not. He couldn't be that dumb... could he? What man with a woman waved her in front of a bull-minded stranger like a red flag to see what would happen? Not a smart man.

But there had to be a solution to this niggling problem of Carrie and Pepper.

The rabbit hunt was another time that Stefan could judge men. He could see who shot their mouths off and who resisted. Of them all, Pepper didn't brag. At all. Pepper. Yeah. Stefan realized he'd always known that Pepper was a superior man and that he was comfortable with the fact. No matter what happened, a man needn't think about Pepper being a gossip.

So. Stefan was supposed to ask advice from... Pepper? Oh, yeah. Sure. Of course.

But there was a bait for Pepper. Stefan could get a discard in the black book for Pepper. He could do that. So he would.

The rabbit shoot was successful, and the outing was invigorating. The jokes were miserable enough to be really funny. And they examined the dead little Peter Rabbits for fleas. Fleas on rabbits meant disease. Stefan said to Pepper, "A woman I know is coming into town Saturday after next. Would you mind showing her around?"

Pepper turned his head slowly and gave Stefan a weighing study. "No. I'd be glad to help out. We doubling?"

Stefan nodded enough to indicate that would be so, but maybe not entirely or not all evening.

Pepper's face was seriously sober as he watched Stefan.

Stefan said easily, "Her name is Trish Willis. She's a nice woman. I've known her casually for some time. Her daddy has the dealership on over east of here, below Bandera."

"That right."

It was a nothing reply. It was only an acknowledgment that something had been said. Stefan knew that. The reply allowed Stefan to either elaborate or quit right there.

Stefan volunteered some more information. "She's a little older than Carrie."

"Yeah?"

"Not much."

Since Stefan didn't continue, Pepper inquired, "She thirty? Forty? Fifty?"

"Now you gotta know, Pepper, that I wouldn't hang a woman around your neck that could pass as your momma."

"No?"

"Nuh-uh. Trish's a shade younger than us."

"How...shaded?"

"Umm. Probably 'bout twenty-seven? 'Round 'bout that."

"I'll see."

"You done promised me."

"I know that."

"Then what'll you 'see'?"

Pepper was logical. "About how old she is. I can't imagine you sharing a young gem with an old friend."

Stefan sighed.

"You serious about Carrie?"

In a low, private manner, Stefan shared the knowledge, "She's not Polish."

Pepper gestured by turning over his empty hand. "There's a whole world out there that's not Polish, and there's places that never even heard tell of that land."

Stefan gasped and straightened. "Now how can you say a foolish thing like that?"

"There are just people who don't get *USA TODAY*. I've heard tell that's so."

In rather elaborate shock, Stefan inquired, "Do you suppose that could be true?"

"It could be possible. Not everyone can live in TEXAS, thereby knowing it all."

Carrie's papa came along and heard the last sentence. He felt called upon to question, "There's people living outside TEXAS?"

And Pepper agreed, "A whole kit and kaboodle."

Pushing it, Mayor Pierce exclaimed, "Now whereabouts are these here strangers you're talking about?"

Pepper decided, "You need a wider scope of the world."

The mayor scoffed, "What? Look past here? This is The Place!"

His neighbor Mr. R inquired with interest, "How much are you paid for those sorts of replies?"

"My yearly salary, meager as it is. It requests my narrow-minded loyalty in forfeit."

Stefan commented, "At least you don't have to give Carrie in sacrifice."

"Her mother wouldn't allow it."

Stefan took his one gutted rabbit home and gave it to Mac. Mac then went into a long dissertation on cooking a skinned rat in the South Pacific in World War II, and adding all sorts of vegetation they didn't know about but what seemed edible. They all got sick.

Stefan said stonily, "It was the rat."

Mac was kind. "That was never settled." Then he guffawed and hit Stefan in the ribs with an elbow. "Get it?" He waited. "Our... *stomachs* never settled!"

Stefan went out and got into his Jeep and left. He went to Carrie's house, although it was still owned by her parents. She was not there. He went to the TV station, and she was out on assignment. They weren't sure where. He went out the door and stood there three minutes, then opened the door and went back inside—as she came out of the ladies' room.

She lifted her eyebrows in a questioning manner, and he growled, "You avoiding me?"

"I'm not a coward. I confront any distasteful situation."

So he took hold of her arm and said to the nearest employee, "She's going to see a possibly stupendous situation."

"Need a camera?"

"I have one," Stefan said over his shoulder as he shoved her before him out of the entrance door. Of course, ladies were supposed to go first, and she did, but he didn't let go of her arm.

"What is this?" Her voice was snippy.

His sly eyes noted that her chest shimmered with the Stefan-forced rapidity of her steps. He told her, yet again, "You are a nuisance."

"Then why don't you leave me alone?" She tilted back her head as she looked up at him. She was not watching where he was pushing her, so she obviously trusted him to see to her safety. "Well? Why don't you?"

"Why don't I what? Throttle you? That's a real possibility."

"My daddy, my brother and my sweet mother would not take your throttling me at all well."

"I'd stuff your body behind the loose brick—"
Hell, why had he said—

Skidding to a stop, she exclaimed, "So *that's* where it is."

Knowing full well, he asked, "What?"

"Your black book of names and phone numbers. It wasn't anywhere that I could see."

"That you could what?"

"See?"

As he thrust her into his car, he asked, "What would you see? I don't have a black book." He lied.

"All men do." She settled herself in his car. She didn't seize the opportunity to escape as he went around to the driver's side. Not until he sat on his seat and was lifting his other leg inside. Then she pushed open the door with full body effort just like it was a warehouse door, and she put one foot out onto the asphalt.

Predictably, he took hold of her arm up by her armpit and jerked her back so that the back of his hand was pushing into her breast. He reached across and pulled the door closed as he said in a low, serious breath, "No." Then he punched the driver button that locked all the doors and he put the key into the ignition.

As he started his car, he looked over at her in a deadly way and said, "Behave."

How come men who are misbehaving, and are being clear out of hand, always say that to a woman? It's one of those things a woman can ponder on—endlessly—in idle time. There is no known answer. They just do it.

Stefan said nothing else but drove deliberately and with firm purpose...to his house. He didn't stop in front. He went to the back of the house and turned the car behind the screened porch. It could not be seen from the road. Interesting.

He was smuggling her in the back way? She sat still as he went to the door and waited. She didn't move, so he came and opened her door and handed her out. Actually, he reached into the car and took hold of her opposite arm in an ungentlemanly way and pulled her out.

Well, Mac was there. She looked around in an airy manner and commented on how tacky the backyard was and that the bushes behind the garage needed trimming.

He did not respond. He waited with great enduring patience, looking down at the steps and breathing in a measured way. But he followed her closely as she mounted the back steps to the screened porch.

She went inside with confidence, since Mac was there. But *was* Mac there? She turned to her captor and questioned, "Where is Mac?"

"Asleep."

She stood patiently and waited as she watched Stefan. He looked a little worn. He looked as if he hadn't slept much. Maybe he was deteriorating? He needed a haircut.

She lifted her hand and slid her fingers into his hair to smooth it back.

His regard came intensely to her and he breathed. He'd probably been breathing all along, but now she could hear it. He groaned and said, "What am I to do about you?"

And she smiled.

He took her against his hard body and held her as he breathed. He'd never been so silent or so agitated.

Carrie was careful. She acted as if he was an unknown animal and she couldn't be sure what he might do.

Six

Feeling in control, Carrie walked from the porch into the kitchen. Mac had to be around somewhere. She called, "Mac?"

In an almost terse voice, Stefan explained, "No one else is here. We're alone."

She turned back and considered him. She said an empty "Oh." Then she just stood there, still.

He breathed some more. Then he asked, "Want some coffee?"

Carrie looked at the empty stovetop, then over the cluttered countertops and back to Stefan. She said, "Please." It would give him something to do. It might even distract him enough that his breathing would stabilize. Maybe not.

He walked to the doorway that led into the dining room and looked back. He said, "The coffeepot's in the sink. The coffee's on the first shelf over the stove."

And having given good directions to her, he left the kitchen and went out of sight.

Carrie listened with deliberate calm. She heard his steps go through the dining room and up the stairs. She felt a stillness spread inside herself. Just what was he doing with her? Well. Nothing. Yet.

In rather vacant, zombied motions, Carrie assembled the coffeepot and began to measure some coffee into the basket. She didn't drink coffee very often. What was she doing?

She was giving herself busy work until she could know what was going on and why she was there. She had been woman-napped by a man whom she knew. He really hadn't given her any choice at all. And no one at the TV station would sound the alarm. They were too busy to pay much attention, and they felt very comfortable with Stefan.

She was alone in an empty house clear out there. She was wearing high heels and stockings that cost twenty-five dollars. The roadway was a common, both ways, two-laner. She could not walk beside the highway in the brush in those shoes and wearing those stockings. She did not have the keys to Stefan's car.

She was helplessly in Stefan's clutches. She smiled a little.

And her glance was caught by the silent, waiting telephone. Hmm. Well, Stefan had probably torn the cord from the wall. When? Well, it could be out of order. She would just assume that it was.

She listened to the sounds Stefan was making upstairs. It sounded as though he was making his bed? If he was changing the sheets, this woman-napping he'd maneuvered was impulse and not planned.

He'd been determined when he'd come to the station. What had set him off? He was so grim about it. No light laughter, no courting gestures or speech. Not even a box of candy. He was not smooth.

But he had dated rather extensively. He had a black book, and he'd talked about a loose brick—*in the fireplace!* She listened, and he was still upstairs. It sounded like he was cleaning the bathroom? It would take him a while to do a good job of it.

Carrie bit her lip and—almost—wished her mother was there to share the amused glances these preliminaries deserved.

So.

He was going to seduce her on clean sheets in a tidy bed with a pristine bathroom? All done on impulse as she waited below. How very droll. How did he know that she wouldn't use his very own defenseless phone and call a cab? It wouldn't be any time at all that everyone in Blink would know that Carrie Pierce had called for a cab from Stefan's house...and his car was there at the time.

How could she walk out on such an earnest man who paid attention to details? Clumsy. Unsubtle. But...therefore unpracticed. However, with him so earnestly distracted, this was the opportunity to see if he really did hide his black book in the bricks of the fireplace. She tiptoed into the living room and approached the fireplace.

None of the bricks moved. She became so engrossed and irritated with failure that she was quite concentrated. Didn't every fireplace have a movable brick?

From behind her on the stairs, she heard Stefan's voice say, "I gave the book to Pepper some time back."

Squatted before the bricks, her hands on them, she stilled, trying to figure how she could alibi out of being caught snooping. As her brain raced, she turned her head, looking back over her shoulder before she asked, "What book?"

But then she forgot what the subject of the confrontation was because Stefan was wearing a terry bathrobe, and his feet were bare at the bottom of his hairy legs. He was naked?

There was a long silence. Then gruffly Stefan said, "I want to show you something."

To hide her humor over his words, she turned back to the fireplace and was still. He wanted to show her something? Her teeth bit into her lower lip so that she didn't laugh out loud. He was not very experienced. Well, neither was she.

However, maybe he wanted to show her how neat it was upstairs. In his robe? Sure.

He came on down the stairs and approached carefully as his tender, rather hoarse voice assured her, "It'll be all right."

He held out his hand helpfully to assist her in rising. So she did put her hand in his. On her own, she stood up and faced him. Her humor had vanished as she looked into his very serious blue eyes.

His breathing was broken, and he kissed her. It was not a beginner's kiss. None of his kisses had ever been awkward. He could really kiss. There was just the possibility that he might not be the innocent she had assumed.

As he kissed her so skillfully, she considered that, actually, he was very bold to bring her there and go upstairs and prepare his bed for her seduction. How shocking that he'd been so confident she wouldn't run away!

With the sly power of his kiss, her knees wobbled. She leaned against the solid rock of his braced body but shifted so that she could get closer.

While she was so distracted that she didn't notice it, she'd put one foot on his bare toes. Stefan did briefly notice. His arms were around her quite tightly, and he lifted her just a little, freeing his foot.

Then he, too, lost contact with reality, with the here and now. He pulled out all the stops as he relinquished all of the ragged, scrambled restraints he'd lived with around this wicked, nubile woman. He really kissed her, and his hands moved up her sides to the rounds of her squashed breasts.

Her breaths changed as they became uneven and louder. She breathed through her mouth, and her hands were restless on his shoulders and into his hair. She seemed almost ready to say things, but they were never said. She encouraged his kisses as she moved and shifted, trying to get ever closer.

She was rubbing against him. Hadn't she been indignant when he had tried to rub against her?

As a victim of a rampant seduction, she wasn't a whole lot of trouble. Stefan lifted her in his arms and carried her upstairs.

He could do that because he'd been carrying sixty-pound sacks of grain around for five months. He'd started with just one sack, grunting as he'd wrestled it. It had taken more time than he'd anticipated before he could add more weight, but he could now lift a seemingly weightless Carrie.

How very flattering to her that he didn't stumble... or sag... or have to put her down. Had that happened, she'd have had to blatantly walk up the stairs to her own seduction. He was a very smart man. He carried her as he would a feather. It was thrilling. She could pretend she'd had no choice.

Men are naturally crafty and sly.

His room was pristine. Well, the bed was. And he put her down on it. He had to stop and look at her to realize she was actually there. There in his bed... for him.

How had this dream materialized? It was real. She was really there. She had not once protested. She had waited downstairs. And she wasn't struggling or protesting.

He took off her shoes and set them on the nightstand. She didn't object. She lay on her back with her hands by her shoulders, palms up with the fingers curled. She watched him with big eyes and a very serious face. She didn't know to move her body or slyly lick her lips or lower her lashes. Her eyes were wide open and quite serious.

He smiled at her gently. Men did that, too. It made the woman think he was harmless.

But then a car drove in the driveway! The two lovers froze. Their eyes met and they stared at each other as their ears listened on beyond. Someone was there? Stefan's car was in back. He was probably home. He could have gone somewhere in someone else's car?

They heard voices. Mac's voice. He was home? Good gravy!

Carrie shot off the bed, taking her shoes off the stand as she went past Stefan, out his bedroom door and down the stairs. She was so fast, Stefan simply stared after the female whirlwind.

Then he looked on the love bed, and his heart squeezed in grief. He straightened it; then he took off the robe and looked down. Poor thing. And he stolidly set about dressing.

The best laid plans of mice and men ... Yeah. He continued to dress. No one ever realized how tough men had it in this bleak, old world.

Mac came inside the house to find Carrie sitting in one of the living-room chairs, casually looking at a *Field and Stream* magazine. Her breaths were a little high. She breathed through her slightly parted lips.

That alerted Mac. He heard his ride back the car onto the road and take off. He listened more carefully and realized Stefan was upstairs. Mentally, Mac hit his forehead with the heel of his palm. He'd loused up his host. How could he mend the bridge? Damn.

In the meanwhile, he spoke only a greeting to Carrie and walked on through to the kitchen to get an unneeded drink of water. Then he went on out the back door and on past the garage, out of sight. There was no way, at all, to erase his blundering intrusion.

Stefan had heard it all. From the top of the stairs, he questioned Carrie in a subdued, roughened voice, "It was Mac?"

Coolly, Carrie replied, "Yes."

Uh-oh. Quick as he could neatly do it, Stefan finished dressing. He came down the stairs in a clean shirt and escorted Carrie out to the car. He stopped before he got in on his side and called, "Mac?"

There was no reply.

Stefan got into the car and backed up at a conservative pace. He went down the drive to the road, turning with leisure, as if not in any hurry and without any weight on his conscience causing him to rush to get her out of there.

Stefan couldn't think of anything more to say, and there was silence on the other side of the front seat of the car. Carrie had no experience in a foiled affair and had no idea how to handle it. She was embarrassed and felt very awkward. She looked out the car window.

She was also disappointed. How strange to feel awkward with a man when she'd almost had sex with him. No, it wasn't just sex, he was going to make love with her.

Love? She slid her eyes over and peeked at Stefan. He was very serious as he watched their way along the scant traffic. He lifted a hand at a call from the curb, and they drove on beyond.

Carrie considered how well known and how respected Stefan was in the town of Blink. And she finally considered how appalled Mac had been. She said to Stefan, "Mac will be so embarrassed."

Stefan was surprised with her words. First, that she could bring herself to speak to him in those awkward circumstances and then, that she could think beyond herself. That proved he really didn't know her very well, but he was enormously pleased by her concern for Mac. He glanced over at her and said, "I probably love you very much. Maybe too much."

And *she* replied, "We'll see."

Since the rock-bottom, basic form of love was sex, that sounded a whole lot like she was saying they'd still get together, and soon. That she said they would "see" was an intense aphrodisiac, and he groaned in mortal anguish.

She was alarmed. "Are you hurt?"

He replied, "Hurting."

"What happened?"

And he turned his head enough to see her before he again watched the road, but he told her very seriously, "You happened to me."

He hadn't yet told her he loved her. So far, all's he wanted was to get inside her clothing. To complain now about her "happening" to him might be an aphrodisiac to him, but to her it was exhilarating! He had admitted that he was partial to her. That she bothered his libido. While that wasn't the love she wanted from him, it was a more serious beginning.

Knowing that, gave her a confidence in herself that she hadn't experienced ever before. She felt she had a handle on him. Then she smiled over the words, and she finally laughed.

Somewhat sour and disgruntled, he asked, "Now what could be funny at a time like this?"

She blushed scarlet, but she laughed.

He was tolerant. He smiled along with her and said, "With me this needy and frustrated and disgruntled, you ought to share something that can make me laugh, too."

Since she'd already just about shared herself with him, that set her off and she laughed out loud.

"Come on," he coaxed. "Tell me what's so funny."

"I can't. I'd shock you. I don't know you well enough to use those words in that meaning with you."

"Sure you can."

"Oh, no. I'd seem like a—" Well, she was! She just didn't want to out-and-out admit she was. Lamely but still smiling, she said, "I can't. Maybe another time."

His curiosity was rampant. "Are you making fun of me?"

And she sobered to say seriously, "Oh, no, Stefan, it's not about you. It's just words. Please. I can't tell you now. I'd burn up with embarrassment."

So he gave her an alternative. "Write them down to tell me another time. I'm so curious what could make you laugh . . . now."

"Write them down!" She was so shocked! "What if someone read them! I'd be scandalized!"

He slowed and kept turning his head to look at her. "Do you have a wicked sense of humor?" He pretended to be aghast at the very thought of such a flaw. But he smiled a beginning amazement.

"I don't think so."

"Tell me. Let me be the judge."

She gasped. "No! I couldn't tell anybody! Don't coax."

"I'll bribe you. I'll get you enough rabbit skins to wrap you in." He could easily get her all those rabbit skins.

"Bunny skins? How could you?"

"Uh-oh."

But she then asked snippily, "Where are you taking me?"

And he explained with tender seriousness, "I need a kiss. A sweet, private kiss."

She went scarlet from her hair roots to her toes. She felt it. "You've had your share for today."

"I haven't, either. I need a kiss so's I can let you out of the car. If you kiss me enough now, I won't demand one at the station."

She finally really looked at him and said soberly, "You can't kiss me at the station."

So, of course, he replied, "See? I'm being considerate. You can kiss me now." He drove onto a nothing track that had a minimum of scattered gravel, and he eased behind some trees.

She was surprised and said, "I didn't know this was here. How'd you know about this place?"

And he lied, "I just saw it."

"Yeah." How could she get so much disbelief in that one word.

He protested with an innocent face, "I did. I was looking for a place we could use while you gave me a decent goodbye kiss without anyone gawking at us."

She might have believed him. She watched around as he stopped the car and turned off the ignition.

She was saying, "You don't have to turn off the mo—"

But he kissed her. He released the catch on his seat and pushed it back as he unbuckled her seat belt. Then he pulled her across his body and he kissed her a little more. His hands moved and he kissed her really, really seriously.

She touched one finger to his great-grandmother's gold ring that dangled in his pirate ear, and she became a malleable mass.

And his hands did maul her. The pirate rearranged her clothing, and he did all sorts of gropings. He was a scandal! And she gasped and was shocked. But he just kissed her again, and she forgot what had startled her so.

By then she was a limp rag, and he was a tensed mass. He put her back on her side of the car and started to adjust his seat. But then he looked at her and groaned.

She frowned, trying to remember if he'd been hurt, and she couldn't think of anything that might make him groan that way. But her mush mind pondered it.

He pulled his seat into place and got the engine started and backed onto the feeder road; then he went on toward the TV station to deposit her. He said, "You ought to straighten your clothes."

She was astonished to see how twisted and disheveled she was. She squirmed and readjusted, and even her stockings were askew.

He almost went crazy trying to watch her and drive, too.

She looked into the mirror on the sunshade and gasped. She pawed through her purse, trying to remember what it was she needed; then she found the comb and combed her short hair. Then she put on lipstick.

To help her, he drove at a snail's pace. That way he could watch her, more. She was fascinating.

It occurred to Stefan: maybe he wouldn't have been so zonked by women if he'd had sisters. He could have gotten used to seeing females, and listening to them would have clued him in to their mind. That way females wouldn't seem so magical and unique. It was all his parents' fault. He should have had sisters.

He said, "I'll go in with you."

She was startled and gave him a quick look. "No."

"I don't want anybody asking where you've been. I'll tell them Mac wanted to tell you a story. He did, but it won't fit in with the flying saga we're getting set up with him and Jerry."

"Nobody over seven years old will believe that."

Stefan was patient. "Maybe not, but they won't be sure. Sit still. I'll get you out." He exited the car and went around to open her door.

She put a high-heeled, shoe-shod foot out on the gravel and lifted her nose to look down it. "Why don't I just say that your hasty seduction plan went awry?"

"It was the initial assault," he corrected with courtesy as he took her hand and helped her out of his car. "You did it very well, considering the last-minute adjustments you had to confront. Next time, plan ahead."

His eyes looked naked as he urged, "You want to try again?"

"I'll have to see." Her voice was a bit formal, but her smile gave him courage. Then she said, "You can lift me and carry me wonderfully. Were you ever a lifeguard?"

"No. I've been practicing with a sack of corn."

She loved it. She looked down her body and repeated, "Sack...of...corn?"

"A man does as he has to do." He looked down her body, then at the sky and finally at his watch and exclaimed, "It's lunchtime. Let's go and I'll get you a sandwich."

She smiled at him again as she walked past him into the building, and she said, "Great. You go get it and bring it back here. I've got to catch up."

So Stefan brought Carrie two sandwiches, milk, cake and a banana. Under the noise of the office, he could explain, "I need to see if it was just testosterone that got you off the floor or if my muscles can handle you in the ordinary flaccidity of unstimulated strength."

She considered. "You can be around me and be . . . unstimulated?" And her eyes teased him.

She shocked him a little, but it was the stimulating kind of shock. She understood that she was alluring to him. Hell, she was alluring to any normal man. Very gravely, he replied, "I have hope that the time will come when I can look on you with depleted regard."

Again she laughed, but she blushed.

With the car phone, Stefan called the lot, and of course Manny replied, "Cisco's."

"How's it going?"

"Well, Stefan, you're running around the territory with that strawberry-haired fluff and—"

"How'd you know that?"

"Linc, Terry, Bill, Movah— You name it, they saw you. But I've sold three cars this morning. Two more and I've topped your daily record. Stay home. Uhh . . . you take her back to work yet?"

"'Course."

"You coming out here yet?"

"Naw, I gotta talk to Mac. I'll be in later."

"Good. I might make top-seller."

"You could, anyway. You're a good man."

"Ah, Cisco, you take a man's legs out from under him, being kind thataway."

Stefan replied, "I'll be in later." And he disconnected the contact. So he could take a man's legs out from under him with compliments? Well then, it ought to work with a woman. Right? All's he said to Manny was that he was a good man. If he told Carrie she was a good woman... she'd probably behave.

Women were very strange creatures. They baffled men. There were men who boasted they knew women and that women would eat right out of their hands. But those men were wealthy first, then good-looking, they moved well and generally they could dance. He put the sun visor down and looked at his reflection in the mirror.

He wasn't that bad. His problem was that he was selective. He'd discarded Carrie because she didn't appear interested in allowing him any privileges, but—

She hadn't shunned him. She'd come over when Mac was there to chaperon. Maybe she wanted commitment? But if Mac hadn't blundered back at such a crucial time, he'd have gotten her that very morning. Uncommitted. Verbally uncommitted.

He groaned in sympathy with his male parts, which were so frustrated, anguished and needy. But he wondered if he had been able to convince that brown-eyed budding woman to give in to him, would she have next shown up with her daddy carrying a shotgun?

Was he ready for commitment?

N-n-not yet.

He just wanted to make love to Carrie. He had serious feelings for her. It was logical to find out if she was somebody he wanted around permanent. It could be she'd be picky and cold and—

She hadn't kissed cold. Her body had been hot and pushy. Her breasts had swollen and loved his hands. She'd pressed and rubbed—

He couldn't drive and think about that. He'd passed his own house. He had to pull the car off into the weeds, turn around and go back to it.

He drove into the uneven, rocky driveway with healthy weeds growing down the middle. He stopped at the front door and got out. He stood and stretched his poor, needy body and looked glumly at the weeds' growth beyond the mowed part. The trees were a variety of mesquite, hackberry, pecan and oak.

The house was big enough.

Having grown up in a big family, it had been lonely living by himself. He liked having Mac there, except for that very morning. They needed some signals.

Stefan walked up to the front door and went inside. Blink doors were only locked by women who didn't want men to come inside after them. Look at Carrie. Twenty-two and still living at home. She ought to have a place by herself.

If she did, would she go inside and hook the screen door, just like she did at home? Until that day she had been a dedicated holdout. How come she had been willing enough that morning? Had that been a rash impulse? Would she try again? Or would she back off at the last minute? Had he just lost the chance of a lifetime that very day?

Knowing how susceptible he was, would she now tease and taunt and...not? Men had it especially rough.

Stefan called, "Mac?"

And Mac came in from the back porch. He stood in the kitchen door and looked across the dining room at Stefan. His jeans waistband was under his stomach. His gray hair was in carelessly perfect curls around his head in a halo. His face carried the years as if all had been in learning. He told Stefan, "I'm sure to goodness sorry." His voice sounded old and wavered a little.

"No problem." *No problem!* He's just told Mac that intrusion at a crucial time in Stefan Szyszko's life was—no problem!

Mac asked, "You want me to move out?" His voice had the uncertainty of a discarded, unneeded old man.

"Hell, no." Stefan had denied it! What was he saying? Why couldn't he just tell this old man to get lost? He said, "We still have the shoot with Jerry to do." That could be a good basis for a time limit on this lingering guest.

"Yeah." Mac brightened a little. "We're committed to that." His confidence came back a little stronger. He had the excuse to stay a while longer. "That Carrie is worth the nuisance of courting her."

Stefan said a disgruntled, "I know."

Mac laughed heartily. "Of all people, you would know that."

But Stefan replied sadly, "Not yet."

Seven

After that, the old man Mac, who was Stefan's alleg-edly temporary guest, did not do anything to alter his slow domination of Stefan's household. The pinochle games continued at Stefan's kitchen table. The old man cooked and shopped. Stefan mentioned things he'd like to eat, and Mac cooked them. Mac kept the house clean. And he slyly became a fixture.

One that Stefan accepted.

With all the burden of routine household responsi-bility off Stefan's shoulders, anyone would think he had it pretty good. But Stefan was in the doldrums with Carrie. She went with Stefan to lunch, she came by his house quite freely. But every damned time she did, Mac was there.

Stefan managed to sneak in sizzling kisses here and there, but it was always too fast and too quickly finished. There wasn't the leisure—ever—for even a good, quick seduction.

He hurt.

He was honed. He was thin and he rarely smiled. He was serious and he slept poorly.

His male friends grinned wickedly at him and asked, "Carrie giving you a . . . hard time?"

So the weekend came that Stefan had gotten a blind date for Pepper. The blind date was the daughter of one of Stefan's car-dealer friends. Her name was Trish Willis, and she was a looker. She knew of Pepper and was animated enough. Trish was Stefan's lure to get Pepper's interest distracted from Carrie to another woman, and then Pepper could leave Carrie alone and forget about her.

However, Pepper showed up with a *woman* whose name was Lois and *another man!* The stranger was from Fredricksburg and looked a whole lot like Mortimer Snerd or, maybe, *MAD* magazine's cover boy, Alfred E. Neuman. The intruder's name was Clem. The name fit. He looked like a real hayseed.

Stefan stared at Pepper with indignant, grimly narrowed eyes. Pepper indicated Lois and had the gall to say, "I'd forgotten I had this date when you dangled Trish under my nose. I knew she and Clem would hit it off. Clem's special."

And Trish, who was *supposed* to latch on to Pepper, was entranced by Clem!

There's just no accounting for taste. But looks can be deceiving. Clem was a man of unusual charm and intelligence. Trish hung on Clem's words and laughed at his jokes—and damned if Clem wasn't a dancer!

Obviously, Clem's mother had looked at her child and realized he'd never make it without help. And she'd been smart. Clem not only could dance, he showed Trish off with his slick dancing ability. And other women came over to beg Clem to dance with them!

Mothers are real smart. Especially when their off-spring are wise enough to cooperate.

Clem told the intruders, "Right after the next ten dances. I'm promised." But he danced with Trish.

Pepper was with Lois, who wasn't trying for Pepper. He was easy with her and even danced with her. They were not enmeshed. Anybody watching knew that.

However, when Pepper danced with *Carrie*, Stefan's jealous eyes saw that they were close together, earnest, talked a mile a minute and hardly moved at all! What was Pepper saying to Carrie, and what was she so busily replying? Neither one laughed. Their talk was not humorous or casual.

What were they saying so intensely? It was as if they plotted. Plotted . . . what? They would run away and have a mad relationship? Elope? For the first time in his life, Stefan felt beleaguered and without skilled backup. The lack wasn't in support from his brothers and kinfolk, the lack was in himself.

During the evening, naturally, the participants danced the TEXAS two-step. Crossing, side-stepping, turning, hip right, hip left, turn left, turn right, the vine, swim down, heel twist, stomp and clap. Yaaa-hooo!

Clem and Trish were the hands-down best there. Wouldn't you know?

When the evening was unendurably over, and they'd all said good night, Stefan drove Carrie to her house, which was the Pierces' house, and asked her, "What was Pepper saying to you, all that time?"

Carrie inquired with interested helpfulness, "What time was that?"

"Whenever you danced."

Carrie shrugged wonderfully. "Probably we were just gossiping."

"About who?"

She lifted empty hands and replied, "Mr. Phillips's cow?"

In a deadly pushy way, Stefan inquired, "What about Phillips's cow?"

Carrie replied. "It got out of the shed and went for the bull?"

"Yeah?"

She confirmed it, "Yeah."

"I mean, what happened?"

Carrie explained logically and shrugged. "The cow ran the bull off."

Stefan nodded because he didn't know what was needed as a reply.

The only good thing about the evening was that Stefan did get to take Carrie home, alone in his car. About midway, he found an isolated place and parked with the car lights off. It was a wearing thing that in a town like Blink there was no privacy to be found anywhere. Whatever was done was observed and discussed.

So the isolated places a man could take a woman were changed often because they became known so fast. Stefan and Carrie were then in such a place with a bandanna over the light of the ignition keyhole.

Their kisses were passionate and his hands undisciplined, but she would not allow him any serious contact. She would say, "We can't stay parked here. Everybody in the county knows this car." She would say, "Umm," and, "Ahhh." She would say, "No!" and, "Good grief, Stefan, you know better!" And she would say, "Let go."

And at her house, which was also occupied by her parents, she hooked the screen door and said, "Good night. I had a wonderful time."

Stefan was ready to lose his mind and join the Foreign Legion. *Was* there still a Foreign Legion?

Men in olden days had it easier. They could go West. In this day and age, there was nowhere for a man to go and not be around women. He couldn't even run away to be a cowboy since he was allergic to horses, and anyway, there were lady cowboys.

How could a woman be a cow-boy? He pondered that. Because cows were female? Did that make the males bullboys?

In this time, women did whatever they wanted to do. Take Carrie, for example. She loved having him frantic, but she could control what all he did. She called the shots. She was a dictator. Dictatress? The female version. She was unbending.

Stefan would sit in a blue slump and consider what could have happened that day if Mac hadn't shown up at that exact time.

Mac most surely did owe him. And Stefan sank down into a long decline.

Everybody was asking, "What's the matter with Stefan?" Well, not everybody. The men all knew.

Carrie told Stefan, "Everyone is concerned about you. What's the matter?"

He looked at her and wondered if any woman could be that dumb and unknowing. He said, "I need you."

And not being at all experienced, and unfamiliar with common terms, Carrie replied earnestly, "We're all here for you. Is your business in decline? With all the cars sold, I don't see how that could be. What are you doing with your income?"

"The business is fine. I don't gamble with money."

"Then, what's the matter?"

"It's you. You're stingy and mean."

She laughed.

A heartless woman does that sort of thing.

Pat's filming bunch landed back in Blink the next day. The weather station said the shoot could well be two days later. The weather, the light and the clouds were supposed to all be perfect. So the principals gathered.

The experienced World War II fighter pilot, Jerry, and his wife, Donna, returned and were again staying with the senior Szyszkos. Donna had driven in with her usual wild freedom, scaring the hell out of anyone on the road around her.

Jerry safely flew in. How can a hotshot pilot be safer than a driver?

Everyone necessary was there for the shoot.

Carrie represented the local station, and she again harbored Pat's camerawoman, Minnie Tombs.

Right away, Minnie asked Carrie, "Got him hogtied yet?"

"Not yet."

"Why'r'ya dragging your feet thataway?"

Carrie inquired with lifted eyebrows and great patience, "Did you take cameraperson dialogue, along with how to run the camera?"

"Yep."

Carrie considered, "I believe I'll throw up."
Minnie cautioned, "Not yet."

There were some other attendees who had cameras, but no others had movie cameras. Pat saw to that.

To watch the two World War veterans and hear their conversations and remembrances was wonderful for Pat's group. The shoot was relaxed and easy. The weather held perfectly as it always did in TEXAS, no matter how it came along.

The microphones in the plane allowed taping, which could be cut and reassembled to match the finished film. It all took time.

The pair was filmed endlessly in takeoffs and landings. And they were filmed in flight by carefully careful additional planes. The sky was perfect, the weather was TEXAS weather, who could ask for more?

And the background of the takeoffs and landings clearly showed Stefan's car lot with its signal antique Jeep aloft on a pole. The car lot seemed especially busy because the curious Blinkers pretended to be customers so they could watch the filming.

While Pat spent the nights going over what they had on tape, the others played...mostly at the senior Szyszkos' house. The intruders became native Blinkers, and Mayor Pierce gave them all citizenship. It was hilarious because he gave them the rules to becoming Blinkers. Primarily, they had to learn to blink correctly.

That took a lot of Lone Star beer and practice.

The final night they were shown a spliced rough tape. The Blinkers were a pushover audience and pronounced the rough as just great. The whole experience was worth all the delight and hilarity of Blinker natives for keeping, feeding and sleeping the crew.

The party lasted 'til dawn. It was exhausting. They were all groggy and tired. Their throats were sore from talking, hollering and singing, and their cheeks hurt from laughing so much.

However, during the entire shoot, Stefan had never had one minute alone with Carrie. He'd seen her, been near to her, watched her, even touched her, but they had had no real conversation nor any intimacy at all.

He longed for her. He suffered.

It was during that time when Stefan wrote the potential song. He labored over it at the car lot. It was a dull day, and unfortunately he had no interruptions. He bared his soul.

The poem read:

The time yer gone jis keeps gettin' longer,
The yearning in my heart jis keeps gettin' stronger,
I'd fly to see ya if I had wings,
But I'm sittin' here chewin' t'baccky and pickin' this gitar's strings.

Ah'm as lonesome as a skunk-sprayed dog,
Miserable as an ain't-got-a waller hog,
My eyes are dried out, beet red, all I do is cry,
If ya ain't back soon, ah'm gonna crawl under a rock an' die.

He added: "This is sung to the tune of 'If the faucet's drippin' and the roof's leakin', I must be home.'"

* * *

Carrie found the letter in her mail and ripped it open. She read it three or four intense times, her breathing hyper, and she held it against her heart and cried, but she smiled the entire time. When her face finally showed no traces of her emotion, she drove over to his house. It was evening. He was home.

Carrie drove to the back of his driveway and discreetly parked her car. She knew Mac was not there. He'd gone with Pat to San Antonio to watch the film-cutting. Stefan would be alone. All alone...

Carrie got to the screen door and lifted her hand to knock, and Stefan opened the door. Actually, the door was already open, she just hadn't noticed, but she looked up and there he was!

He couldn't believe she was really there. He reached out, pulled her into his house and closed the door with the sound of the sealing of a pharaoh's tomb. Then to be really sure it was Carrie, he kissed her.

She did respond. She even put her arms around him. Then she moved her head back, but only so that she could breathe somewhat, and she noticed how worn he looked. He was ill? She put her hands to his head. He felt hot.

He was acting quite strange. His breathing was raspy, his eyes were intense and he shivered.

She asked, "Are you all right?"

And he replied, "Soon." Then he kissed her again. She was a trifle disoriented. She'd thought they were on the screened back porch, but they were on the stairs. That surprised Carrie.

After the next kiss, she discovered they were in his room. She looked around quite surprised. She was boggled by his kisses, anyway. And so her disorientation wasn't odd. She looked around rather vaguely. How had they gotten there?

He was trembling, so she thought he must be very tired and ill. She asked, "Do you need to get into bed?"

And he replied very positively, in an uneven voice, "Yes."

So she helped him to undress. She was a little distressed that he shivered. But he was so hot to touch, he must be feverish?

She looked at him with some concern, and discovered she was standing in her garter belt and hose with her shoes on, *and that was all!*

She lifted her hands and put them—one on top of the other—between her soft, round, naked breasts and said in some astonishment, "My goodness."

And he said, "Yeah." For whatever that could mean.

She saw that he was taking his trousers off his feet. He needed to get into bed; he was that ill. He probably needed her to warm him? She asked him, "Do you have a hot-water bottle?"

He shook his head. He was concentrated on getting her into his bed.

As he completed undressing, she turned away from him to lean over as she pulled back the covers. Behind her, he moaned and gasped. And she turned back to find him right there in front of her.

His hands were everywhere. He probably didn't know how to get her into bed with him. She lifted the covers and said, "How can I help you?"

And he grinned very widely and said, "There's no need. I'll do everything."

It was then her logic kicked in, and she suspected he was not ill at all but was only in dire need of her body. Well. Okay. She could do that. She smiled at him and put her arms around him.

He kissed her until she felt her eyeballs swirl. He bent her back over his arm, and his big hand slid over her naked breast and then down over her hip and around onto her bottom. Seemingly he did that all at once.

She gasped.

He got her shoes off because she insisted, and he put her into his bed. She still wore the garter belt and stockings. Those retained items gave her a sense of modesty. She didn't feel that she was entirely naked since she still wore those coverings.

Women are odd.

He got into bed with her, crowding her. He made such hungry sounds. He ran his hands so gently on her body, and he groaned as if in exquisite pain and his gasps were getting hoarse. That worried her. And gently touching his great-grandmother's earring, she voiced the question he quoted for*ever* afterward. "Are you," she asked, "are you in pain?"

And he agreed ardently, "Yesss!"

She melted in compassion. "Oh, you poor thing. How can I help? Is it a headache?"

"Lower." And he almost choked over having to use the word. Even Mac and Jerry had told of all the guys who'd told of using it to neophytes. So he said it again, "Lower."

He continued to beg for her response to the word, and her hand was exquisitely shy, but it did move. Down. She did encounter his anxious sex. And she did touch it. Then she said, "Ahh, so that's the problem."

He agreed in a rough, hoarse groan, "Yesss!"

She asked, "Do you have some...protection for us?"

That stopped him for a minute. To instantly say yes might sound— But then his tongue thought to ask, "Do you?"

"Yes," she replied.

He was boggled. "*With* you?"

"Well...yes." Such a tiny sound.

And he became more agitated. She'd come prepared to assault him? And he'd not waited? Well, if he had waited for her, they would never in this world have made it up there to the bed!

He suggested, "I think it would be a good idea to get one now."

"It's in my purse, downstairs."

He was dead sober, trying to decide if they should use one of his or if he could let her get away from him long enough to go down, get hers and come back upstairs. He could use her fetching the first condom for a long, long time, if she ever got snippy on him.

He asked, "Where's your purse?"

"I'll get it." Then she said, "You have to let go of me."

It came to him that she would have to crawl over him to get to the floor, and he could watch her leaving...and coming back. "I'll go with you."

"Wait here."

But he got up because he desperately needed to move around and distract himself a little. He followed her to the top of the stairs and watched her go to her purse. She took out a *box!* A whole box? He wavered a bit. She seriously brought the box up the steps. She carried it on her palm, holding it out in front of her naked body, which was marked as civilized by a garter belt and stockings.

She was walking stocking-footed.

He was so touched by her serious foray to come to seduce him that he was sobered a little in his wild, sexual seizure. As badly as he lusted for her, he would now make love to her.

And he did.

It helped that the condoms were polka-dotted. All colors. His sex looked like it belonged in a circus. He smiled a lot. She was very serious.

Under his hands, her body was cool and rather stiffened. He coaxed her into relaxing, but she was braced. He found she was a virgin. That slowed him even more. He'd heard tales from guys who'd stumbled onto one and not been prepared to take the time with her.

But Stefan was thirty. This virgin was his first one. He was sweet and loving and careful. And her initiation was exquisitely slow and careful. He coaxed her along with great skill and much loving. Her climax was exquisite.

As they lay replete, she leaked tears, but those were of emotion, and she was very tender with him.

He couldn't remember a bed partner who had reacted so gently with him. Those few times had been either raucous or hilarious or hard driving, but the tenderness was never as exquisite as this time with Carrie.

And his love grew. He said he had a plain, utilitarian condom.

She laughed when he wanted to do it again. She laughed and shook her head and blushed. He showed her his problem, and she was shy. He was so charmed by her. And he was gentle and sweet and didn't insist.

She lay in his arms and asked him, "Where did you find the poem?"

"I made it up. It's not so smooth, but you need to think of the love behind those painful rhymes."

"It's so sweet. Thank you for it."

"Are you going to admit I love you and that you love me?"

"Probably."

"I never had anyone as sweet as you."

She stilled. She knew he was probably experienced, but to have him say such a thing really shocked her.

He had never before had to figure peripheral nuances. He shouldn't have said such a thing.

She asked coolly, "How did I compare to all the others."

"None was—" It was only then he realized how many times his father had said, "Never let any woman know you ever had another woman! Deny it, even if you've been divorced twice and have five kids."

Stefan had blown it. He adjusted his sentence gently, "None was sexual. I'm talking kissing and being around a woman who was talking to me."

"And you've never made love to any woman?"

"I have to be honest with you, I've kissed women before you. I'm thirty. You have to know I have kissed a few."

"But you've never taken them to bed with you, this way?"

"No." Well, that was honest. He'd never before made love to a woman wearing a garter belt and hose.

While wearing a polka-dot condom, he said, "You're my first."

"Why do you have the condoms?"

Logically, he replied, "I got them in San Antonio, so the druggist here wouldn't think I was trying to get you."

She exclaimed, "I did the same thing!"

"You went to San Antonio for those polka-dot condoms?"

"I could have gotten plaid, but I knew you weren't Scotts."

After a nodding pause, Stefan said, "I love you, Carrie."

"I'm amazed how nice it is. I've heard it was, but I couldn't see how it could be that nice."

"Let's try it again."

She blushed and said, "I don't think we should. It seems so... greedy."

Uh-oh. Was she going to be selfish? Shy? Withholding? He looked at his love and wondered, becoming cautious.

She said, "You're rather... big.... I'm a little... sore."

So it wasn't indifference. She was too new to it. He said in a husky voice, "Awww. Here, let me comfort you."

So he petted her and rubbed her stomach in nice, slow swirls and he kissed her throat and fooled around and by golly, he did it again!

She asked, "How come we did this again?"

"Well, you kept moaning and pulling at me so and insisting and struggling with me that I just gave up."

She said, "I don't recall doing all that."

He was incredulous. "You mean I got out of hand and sneaked you?"

"Surely not."

"'Course not! I'm a nice young man, an upright cit— Hush that! A *good* citizen. I wouldn't do a thing like that. You assaulted me."

"Not that time, but I suspect there could come a time when I might."

The air whooshed from his lungs and he fainted, lying pale and lax with his eyes closed.

She was alarmed and leaned up over him. She was anxious and said, "Stefan?"

He opened his eyes a slitted bit and asked in a tinied voice, "Now?" just like he was terrified.

She was so amused.

He grinned and raised up over her to share their humor. She might be as magical as he'd always thought.

She said, "I didn't know making love was having fun, too."

"You didn't know it was fun?"

"I've always seen the hot-and-heavy-breathing upper-body tusslings on film. I've never seen the playfulness. I didn't know a couple could laugh and tease in fun."

He replied to the neophyte, "There isn't any situation that can't be fun. Oh, there aren't many giggles in a murder, but I'm talking ordinary lives and living.

"Once mother told us boys, 'No matter what the circumstances, no matter how deadly or serious it is, if you look for it, there's humor.' No healthy child believes his mother right off thataway, and I'd look for things."

He tilted his head and looked down at her. "Are you old enough to remember when we buried my brother Billy? I thought of what my mother had said and bitterly wondered what was the humor there. At his grave, the priest had us pray for the dearly departed, then those other departed entombed there. I thought they'd had enough help.

"Then he wanted a prayer for himself. I figured he could handle that. But then he requested a prayer for the *next* person who'd die! I slid my eyes around and thought that was a little rude. Then I thought what if it was *me* and, inside, I laughed. So in that terrible time, I had found something to make me laugh. And I looked over at my mother, blowing her nose from crying over Billy, and I knew she was smarter than me."

Carrie nodded sagely, "Parents tend to be mostly right."

Curious, he asked, "What have you found that they were wrong about?"

"They kept telling me to wait for sex."

"And they were right." He was positive.

"This is fun! I should have tried it with..."

She didn't continue, and he demanded, "Who?"

"No one you know. It was a chance encounter."

"No. Those are the worst. You have behaved because you knew I was the man for you. We'll get married and live happily ever after."

"Well, I might like to try out another man or two be—"

"No!"

"Are you selfish?"

"Yes!"

"I thought you were the most generous person I've ever met. How can you be so narrow-minded now?"

"Behave."

She looked around perkily. "Get out of your bed and get dressed."

"No. No. With me, it's okay."

And she laughed. She lay back, crossed her hosed ankles, put her hands behind her head and just smiled, so amused.

He watched her very seriously. He said, "I can't take you again. Yo— I'd get too sore."

She raised up, all compassion, and laid her hand on him. "Have I overused you?"

A man seizes on any opportunity. He replied, "Just about. Mostly. It hasn't been too bad. I'm okay."

"Is it fighting to get free?"

"It's shy and wants to be hidden."

She lay back, laughing.

One thing about an inexperienced woman, everything is new. It was easy to make her laugh.

He turned to her, carefully scooped her against him and just cherished her. He rubbed his face against hers and nuzzled her. He made appreciating sounds.

Living was a miracle.

Eight

Stefan then assumed his bedtime with Carrie was an established fact, and he became relaxed and contented. He smiled at the replete woman and didn't see any reason to hurry into any stern and limited commitment. He was finally, really on the catbird seat. He smiled a lot.

Referring to the permanence known to be said of the bonds of marriage, Stefan told Carrie, "Let's work into this gradually. There's no rush. Let's give the town time to get used to the idea."

Yep. Stefan said exactly that.

Carrie blinked the native blink. In Blink, TEXAS, Stefan thought the citizens should get used to the idea of him courting her? For crying out loud. Who could possibly be surprised? Unprepared?

Then she had the audacity to inquire, "Will you give me your great-grandmother's ring?" It was obviously the ultimate test, and since she'd mentioned it so soon, it was one she had considered.

And just like that, he replied, "No, I'll get you a new one. This is very soft pure gold. It can easily be squashed."

She replied clearly, "I'd like to wear your great-grandmother's wedding ring."

And he gently shook his head as he touched the ring in his ear.

She was offended.

He was logical. "I'll get you another, just like it. This gold is too soft to wear all the time. I'll get you one you can wear."

She retorted, "You aren't committed if you don't want me to have your great-grandmother's ring!"

He was puzzled by her demand. "She gave it to me on her deathbed."

Carrie waited, but he'd said all he intended. She enunciated, "She gave it to you for your wife."

He frowned at Carrie. "I was ten years old. I was just a kid."

She considered him, then she eased negatively from his bed and went to the bathroom. Women tend to do that to give themselves space. In times of confrontation, women need to check their makeup and hair.

When she came back into his room, she was pleasant and allowed him to hold and kiss her and say all the nice things to her, but emotionally she had withdrawn just a tad. She was sweet to him in turn, but... there was a difference.

Over his teasing protests, she left him and began to put her clothing back on. She was sure her car had been in his driveway far too long as it was. She kissed him with very sweet restraint and left him there in that suddenly empty bed.

* * *

Carrie's mother told her only daughter, "If Stefan won't offer you his great-grandmother's ring, he's not ready for permanence. You'll have to be careful. He feel's he's nailed you down already—" that was her mother-radar word choice "—but he isn't ready to take the final leap. He could let this period of the relationship drag on for some time."

"I shouldn't look for a wedding gown?"

Her mother replied, "Not yet. He's adjusting. It would be wise if you weren't too certain he's the one. He could sell out his business and leave town, or something similarly withdrawing."

"How should I handle this?"

Her mother slowly turned her head, looked into her daughter's eyes and said one word. "Stingily."

That was clear enough.

There was no way, at all, that Stefan could get Carrie to move in with him. Besides his being unreasonable about the antique ring, there were the roadblocks of his family, her family, Mac and the neophyte that were all in the way of it.

She was shy, she blushed, she shook her head, she laughed, she teased. While she allowed his kisses and close squeezes, she declined reclining. And while she might touch a pensive finger to the ring in his ear, she never again mentioned wanting it.

She did tell him, "I shouldn't be so intimate with you. You know that. You're terribly personal. Shame on you." She said, "Why, Stefan!"

He said, "You loved it. Let me. I hurt." All those much said complaints.

But they were never again alone for quite an endless while.

It was astounding. How could it happen that way?
To be so close, that close, and now be so far apart even
standing side by side.

She would come to his house and he'd be glued to
her, encouraging her to get hotter, and somebody
would be at the door. Brothers, friends, women, Mac,
it was boggling. They never had five minutes alone.

He could have managed in that brief time space, but
she needed some warming up.

On top of everything else, she was difficult to contact. Why wasn't she sitting by her phone, waiting for
him to call her? When he did call her, she wasn't at
work, she wasn't at her house, her mother said so.
Stefan was annoyed by that. When he ran into Carrie
by the greatest chance, he'd ask her, "Where've you
been?"

She would reply some idiot thing, like once she said,
"Sally Joe had to find some matching thread for a
dress she's making, and I helped." Then Carrie
laughed and asked, "Guess who we saw?"

"Who?" Since she laughed, he grinned and his eyes
sparkled.

Merrily, she responded, "Out on the road with the
hood up on his car... Pepper!"

All the joy went out of Stefan. He said deadly earnest, "Tell me you left him there."

"No. I fixed the hose. I had the tape!" Then Carrie lifted her eyebrows and was smug. "I did the
wrapping." And she added, "Pepper said I was just
perfect."

After that, when he asked her for a date or to meet
him somewhere, she was busy. Or she brought someone along, or somebody joined them. It was never

another man. It was one of her female friends. Who would ever believe the tiny town of Blink, TEXAS, had that many women around loose?

If he wanted her to come over and watch a movie, she'd ask, "Which one?" And no matter what it was, she'd reply in disappointment, "Oh, I've seen that one," or "I've seen it twice. I don't think I could handle a third time," or, "You should have told me you wanted to see that movie. I saw it with Penny."

He never expected her to actually see a film or visit somebody, he just wanted her to come to his house and go to bed. She was never alone with him. It was always another couple or a bunch of people or she was too busy. Her excuse was never a date. There was no other man.

He was smart enough to understand that she wasn't toying with him. She kissed him wondrously. She wrapped her arms around him and made the sweetest sounds. She expected him to make up his mind. To commit himself. He wasn't ready, not for that. Not yet.

He told her she was selfish. She was cold. Actually, she hadn't been at all cold that one time. She'd blistered the paint on his bedroom wall. Had she been faking it?

And with sobering worry, he wondered if he had hurt her. Had he hurt her, and she couldn't face doing it again with him? He felt like a brutish animal.

He asked her, "When we made love, did I hurt you?"

She gave him a sloe-eyed look and smiled as she whispered wickedly, "You ruined me for any other man. How'd you get that good?"

The burden of worry slid off his shoulders, and he grinned at her. "Let's see if it was a fluke."

She only laughed and blushed scarlet. She put her hands to hide her face and scolded, "Don't tempt me that way."

Stefan became more honed. But she wouldn't. Could a woman have that many periods? He checked it out. Then, since it had worked once, he tried for more poetry, but what he wrote just didn't make it, not even with him.

He began to look like a starving poet.

She brought him...food. Could he bring himself to marry and have children with such a flawed, unknowing, un-understanding, selfish woman? Yeah. He'd be brave and cope, if she'd just lie in his bed and let him hold her.

Mac got involved. "How come you and Carrie aren't snuggling anymore?"

"She's trying to get me nailed down."

Mac was astonished. "So?" He put out his arms and flopped them to his sides. "Tell her you're hooked."

"I can't."

Mac was logical, "Then date another woman. Scare her."

But Stefan shook his head. Then he looked into blankness. "I can't see anyone else."

As well as he knew the inevitable finale, Stefan didn't buckle down with any commitment. But he dreamed of her coming to his house and taking off her clothing as she slowly came up his stairs to his room. She'd get into bed with him and her heat would scald his cold flesh—and she'd rip the earring from his ear and say, "Hah! Now you *have* to marry me. I have your great-grandmother's ring!"

He'd awaken and feel his ear. The ring was still there. Why did he hesitate in giving it to her? Was he that unsure she was The One?

Why didn't he say, "You'll get it when we're m-m-m-m—" He found he couldn't actually say the word.

If he couldn't get past the *M* sound, was he a coward? Didn't he want to get married? Well, it had been pretty nice for thirty years not being married. But he did notice how few women his age weren't married.

He'd had to get a woman *eight years* younger than he! That was serious. If he waited another couple of years, all the younger women would be married and his bride would probably be sixteen. Think of trying to teach a child to be an adult.

He'd have to say, "No, you can't watch TV, you have to get that theme done for school." He'd say, "How are the driving lessons going?" And he'd say, "No, you *must* take cooking again next year." What a drag. He needed a woman older than sixteen. Twenty-two was already an irritant.

But he loved Carrie. She was a good and charming woman who did a good deal of work in the community. Besides that luscious body, she had a good mind and great curiosity. He needed to be persistent. How could he get her to be less stingy? His body was going crazy.

But that was no reason to give in to Carrie. She wasn't cooperating. Cooperating? And he remembered how Meg had cooperated. She'd cooperated all right. She'd snared him entirely...and she'd tossed him cheerfully aside. Stefan had thought she loved him, but she'd only used him with great pleasure.

Was he afraid that Carrie would discard him? What was making him so gun-shy? Was he insecure?

He dreamed she came into his room. That she was in that garter belt and those stockings, and she lusted for him. She climbed all over him salaciously and drove him mad. Then she laughed and went away, her laugh trailing after her.

Maybe she would come to him by herself. She hadn't been a cold woman. She would get the itch, sneak over to his house and creep up his stairs and into his bed. Mac would be gone again. She would come. So would he.

He cleaned the house and especially his room and the bath. And she did come over, but she didn't come by herself. She brought along two of her friends, and they all chatted and moved around and laughed a whole lot.

But otherwise she was busy with her job. She was off on all sorts of jaunts with her friends. She apparently didn't even miss being alone with him. She hardly ever called him. When he called, she wasn't there, at her house or office. Before then, he hadn't called that often.

She was sure of him. She'd given him a sample and now she was waiting to reel him in?

He was offended.

She brought him samples of her cooking. She left them there with Mac. Mac bragged on her cooking.

Suspiciously, Stefan asked Mac, "How do I know the dish wasn't done by her momma?"

And Mac replied kindly, "The side is just a little scorched."

Quite formally, Stefan asked Carrie to go with him to dinner one night. It was about five in the evening when he'd called.

But since it was last minute, that way, Carrie was so sorry. She said, "Well darn. We've already got something planned. Why don't you come along with us? You'll be the only man, so I'll have to keep a close watch on those voracious women!"

He did go. The others laughed beyond what would have been normal. Were they calling attention to themselves? Or were they amused that his evening had become so limited by their being around?

He'd drop by her house and either all her family was there, and stayed, or at least one of them was home. They were noticeably around. Not discreetly. He couldn't get in any really wicked hugs or kisses.

He couldn't get her alone.

He asked her. "Don't you want to be with . . . just me?"

She laughed. "I'm a-scared of you. You're so marvelously wicked!"

Rather grimly, he narrowed his eyes and tilted his head. "It was my house and my bed. It was your choice."

"Oops."

Then again vulnerable, he asked, "I didn't hurt you, did I?"

She sobered and put her hand on his chest. "It was . . . wonderful."

"Then—"

But her mother came into the hallway. She said, "Hello, Stefan." She was kind and asked questions of him, and she was . . . there.

His life was one of anguished frustration. And he had dreams that were filled with turmoil and disasters. Carrie would be just out of reach. In his dreams, her reactions were different.

She would be in danger, and he would struggle to get to her. Or she would be hot and wanting and he couldn't get free of something to get to her. Or she would be aloof and turn and just look at him with such adult consideration that she scared him.

She would lie under him and writhe around him like a woman-snake, that wicked and that dangerous.

She would come to his bed and climb all over him. She would love him tenderly and she would love him wildly. She would do all the things ever done to a man... and he would be a little shocked.

Why couldn't she have a little of that attitude in real life? Why did she avoid him? Didn't she care for him at all? How could he have time alone with her? Well, probably because she knew what he wanted.

Didn't she want him? That made him especially melancholy. Maybe she didn't. Maybe he hadn't pleased her.

When she'd been there at his house, and Mac hadn't been around, look at what had happened! And she'd been prepared for making love.

But she wasn't pensive without him. She wasn't serious about not being with him. How was he to figure her?

What could he do that would catch her competitiveness? She didn't feel the need to draw his attention, she was just waiting to reel him in.

Reel him in? The thought made him wonder. He didn't feel like the chaser, the catcher, he felt like a hooked fish.

At his dealership, a woman came in who was a stranger. She wanted a Jeep. She was a twentieth-century woman, independent and assertive. She looked on him with interest.

He was in such a rejected turmoil that he actually asked her to dinner. They sat at a table in a restaurant, *there in Blink!* He said so little and bored her so stupid that she got up and walked out of the place. For some while, he just thought she'd gone to the ladies' room. He did think that. But she was gone out of there.

One way or another, Stefan provided great conversational tidbits to the compact town of Blink. His dad was one of the hilarious perpetrators of the foibles of Stefan.

But Carrie was not amused. Her retort to him when he called was that what was sauce for the gander was sauce for the goose! And she hung up.

Uh-oh.

He sent her flowers. But when he went home that night, they were on his back steps squashed down in a bucket. They had not been handled tenderly.

Stefan sought his dad's advice. He came out to the dealership. Manny was gone for the day. The two males sat and discussed women and their peculiarities and the ways a man could counter such conduct.

Just as an example of how really desperate he was, Stefan asked his very own father, "How'd you get Momma? I hear tell she was something before you got a handle on her."

And his father sighed as does a man with a great burden. "I've been holding men back from her all my life. And still do! She doesn't do a thing! She doesn't flirt or swish or anything.

"Even at the tender age of six years old, she was a caring Polish Mother and the worst kind. Males are drawn to her like flies."

"What'd you do?"

Mr. Szyszko shook his head over the burden of it all. "I persevered. Until we got married, I got in a lot of fights. I was always sore somewheres. I lost weight and the only time I smiled was at her. She was a nuisance. But I won."

"Mr. Rodway said something about that. That you had to chest-crowd any number of guys when you were courting her."

"That's never really stopped. Men tend to know a good thing when they see her." He sighed with drama. "It's aged me considerable. I gotta always be on the alert. That's what'll happen if you nail Carrie. That blond-red hair isn't the only thing that pulls men's eyeballs out thataway."

"We never go out alone now. She's... set herself away from me. She comes by with food for me only when Mac's there."

"Women do that when they're hot for a man. It protects them from theirselves."

"You think so?"

"Yeah. You need to commit to her or let her go."

But when Stefan called Carrie, she wasn't there, she'd just left, or she'd be back in about twenty minutes. It was that same kind of reply at home and at work. And Stefan smelled a Blink conspiracy.

He called his dad out to the car lot again. Since Manny was there, the father and son went out amongst the cars and could talk.

"How come I can't get in touch with her?"

"Because you went out with that woman like the fool you are. You got that from your mother's side of her family, no real Szyszko would have done that *right here in Blink,* for God's sake. You're going to have to do some crawling. She's worth it."

Stefan protested, "How can I crawl, when I can't get in touch with her? Her mother says she isn't home. She put my flowers very unkindly in the slop bucket on the back steps! At the station, they say she's off on some kind of assignment."

"Everybody's having a hilarious time with you, son. They'll see how you take this. It's one of the problems that you confront living in a small area, this-away. The men all love it that some other guy is getting it, not them. But they all love you. There's not enough going on, so *any*thing is interesting. You know that. Don't go into a decline.

"One way or another, this'll be solved. Be patient. Let her know you love her. But if you're not deadly certain about her, don't. Be sure you really want to be committed. Marriage is a very serious business. It should last forever, if you pay attention now."

Then his dad put his hand on Stefan's shoulder and said, "Good luck in convincing Carrie, but be sure she's The One, hear?"

Stefan bobbed his head a little.

His dad watched him a while; then he gently took his heavy hand from his youngest's shoulder. He stood there a while, just being around. He asked, "You okay?" Stefan nodded. Finally his dad walked away.

Stefan sighed and looked out over the TEXAS land and wondered why he was there, at that time, in this world. What did God have in mind for him? Was he supposed to stay right there, struggling in a community that would never change?

He put deep thought into Carrie. How would his life be if he let go of her? How could he "let go" when he didn't really have hold of her? And he thought of his life without her.

He considered other women. None was anything like Carrie. None was as interesting or as sweet or as thrilling as she was. He did love her. And he wanted it permanent.

So.

What was he to do?

Stefan tried to start over fresh with Carrie. He called her. Doggedly. She was never available. He also went by her house, and her mother or daddy or brother was glad to see Stefan, but they said she wasn't around. To try...

Two days later, knowing from her mother that Stefan had talked to his daddy about her, because his dad had told her papa, Carrie answered the phone.

Stefan said, "How about supper someplace?"

She declined.

"What're you going to do that can't be put off?" he asked. "I haven't seen you in a month of Sundays."

"Well, I have a date for that night."

Stefan was appalled! "You dating somebody else?"

"Pepper has very kindly invited me out."

"What do you mean 'very kindly'?"

"You abandoned me...again."

"I haven't been able to find you! Where the hell have you been? What do you mean you're going out with...*Pepper!*" Stefan was really upset.

Carrie was indignant, "You dated that woman!"

Why'd she say that? Well, he'd done it deliberately to make her territorial. She was mad at him and giving it back. He needed to be careful. God only knew what all she might do in revenge. This was serious.

Carefully, Stefan said in an almost normal voice, "So you have a date with...Pepper? Where you going?"

And Carrie said, "He hasn't said."

"We could double."

"No."

She didn't elaborate. She gave him the willies. She hung up.

That night, he hunted for them all over Blink and out into the countryside. And with his breaths high in his chest and his hands trembly in anticipation of a confrontation, he even checked out Pepper's house. But he never found them.

He parked his car down her street and waited all the rest of the night for Pepper to bring her home, but they didn't come there.

With the morning's light, *she came out her front door!* Fresh and bright, she came down the steps and got into her car and backed down the driveway. As she went past his car, she tooted her horn one brief time to acknowledge him...and she drove on away.

So she hadn't had a date with Pepper? She'd just told Stefan that to get him agitated? She'd been successful!

He went home and slept for two hours, bathed, shaved and dressed precisely. He went to her office at the station and asked for her, but she wasn't there. She wasn't anywhere.

He had a hard time finding her. He ran across her in the middle of the street and stopped dead in the road. The cars driving past them held interested citizens and the men all smiled...with empathy.

As the cars passed slowly around the stranded pair, the drivers said things like, "Hang in there." "Don't let her get the upper hand." "If you can't keep her, give her to me." Things like that, which Stefan barely heard because he was so concentrated on the witch.

Stefan demanded, "Carrie, are you sleeping with him?"

"Which one?" she inquired with bright-eyed, exaggerated interest.

She did that! He said through his teeth, "*Anyone?*"

"Why do you ask?"

"I have the right to know?"

"Why?"

"You belong to me."

She laughed as she walked off away from him, leaving him standing alone there in the middle of the street.

Women were a great, thundering nuisance.

Then when Stefan went for solace at his parents' house, Stefan's mother said to him, "You have to make up your mind. She isn't Catholic, you know, and she ought to convert. Have you discussed that with her?"

Stefan asked blankly, "What?"

"Is she going to join our church?"

Stefan asked, "Who?"

His mother was patient with her youngest, who had finally shown that he took after his father and become an idiot. She replied gently to a sublevel mentality, "Carrie."

"Why would she join our church?"

And his mother replied, "Most of us go to just that one church. Will you join another?"

"How do I know?"

His mother responded, "Most people talk part of the time."

"She hardly talks at all."

His mother's eyes flared.

Stefan went on, "When I see her, she's always silent with those big eyes on me, and she waits for me to say something. I ask how she is, and she says, 'Fine.' I ask if she'll come over to supper, and she says, 'Come to our house.' We just spend time together. We don't talk."

"You'd better start talking."

"About what?"

His mother was becoming impatient, "What church you'll join!"

Stefan was annoyed. "I already belong to a church!" His mother ought to know that. Stefan narrowed his eyes as he realized his mother was a *woman*. She was one of *them*.

He left his old home as if he'd washed up on an alien shore... and was alone.

Then Stefan asked Mac, "How long do you intend staying around?"

"You want me to leave?"

Stefan's reply was honest. "I'm just curious."

Mac waited as he pondered; then he replied slowly, "Well, I guess I really don't have any kind of excuse to hang around."

Stefan was looking out the window and not paying much attention.

Mac asked with equal slowness, "Can I stay here until I find me a place?"

Stefan lifted his eyebrows and asked, "Hmm?"

Mac repeated his question.

And Stefan said an indifferent, distracted, "Sure. There's no problem."

Nine

So it shouldn't have surprised Stefan, as much as it did, that Mac went into a decline.

He seemed his age. That was different. He'd been feisty and overbearing for the entire time he'd been around. To find him meek and shuffling was finally attention getting.

Stefan asked, "You okay?"

And Mac rumbled a clogged, "Yeah."

"You're acting . . . fragile."

"I'm a bear. No problem."

Because of his granddaddy, Stefan knew that "no problem" was the reply to anything in World War II. The troops could solve whatever, however, and on time. They'd done that, too. It wasn't just a brag. It was how the sergeant had lived during that time.

Stefan asked, "How come you never remarried?"

"I never met a girl like Carrie."

"Your voice is hoarse." Stefan frowned at his guest.

"It's just a little cough. No problem."

There was that term again. Stefan squinted his eyes.

He called Carrie the next day from the dealership. He said he was Bill Clinton and got her.

She said a snippy, "Yes?"

"I don't think Mac is feeling well."

"Then call a doctor!" And she hung up.

That shocked Stefan. Of course, Mac was his guest and his responsibility. Consulting with a doctor was what he should do.

Then Stefan realized that the reason he'd called Carrie instead, was because she might be concerned and come over to his house to check up on Mac.

She hadn't. She'd only said for him to call a doctor.

Rather discouraged, Stefan called his own doctor. The nurse who was named Phyllis said, "Bring him in tomorrow, Stefan. We're jammed up, but we'll figure a way. It's probably the flu that's going around."

Surprised, Stefan asked, "There's a flu going around?"

"Honey, you're out of touch."

No one had called Stefan "honey" in some time, and he was shocked.

Phyllis asked, "Want to go to the rodeo with me?"

Stefan replied, "Sorry, but thanks for asking."

And she told him, "Keep me in mind."

Stefan hung up gently. "Hmm," he said. He no longer belonged to Carrie? He was back on the open market? Hanging on a spike like dead meat? His self-image wavered. The nurse at his doctor's office thought Stefan was free.

Was he? Had Carrie rejected him—really? Not just temporarily, but permanently? Had she passed out the word that she'd discarded Stefan Szyszko? And he was depressed.

That night after supper, he got up to go outside and walk around his tacky yard for a while.

As he passed by Mac's chair, the old man asked, "You get me an appointment?"

Stefan stopped and looked at Mac. He was an old, discarded man. The only difference between the two was that Stefan was younger.

He leaned over and put a hand on Mac, who at eighty-two was an orphan, and he said, "We all love you. We'll take care of you."

Then Stefan went outside into the early summer's dusk. He considered the possibility he might get the flu and be a tragic victim of the disease, and that aloof Carrie would be shocked to hear he was dying.

She'd rush over to his house and take the stairs two at a time to get to him. She'd kneel by his bed and take his hand to press it against her soft, heaving breasts. Her sweet lips would say, "I didn't mean it. I love you! Say you'll live!" just as he drew his last, shallow, unsteady breath.

She wouldn't be able to accept his death, and she'd cry out to him. She'd wring her hands and wail in anguish—

"Stefan?"

Since the name was on cue, Stefan didn't realize for a minute that it wasn't just inside his head.

He walked along slowly, watching his feet manage that.

With great patience, the voice said again, "Stefan!"

In wonder, he turned around—and there she was!

His lips parted, and he couldn't believe she was there. Had he conjured her? Why would this be so real? If he touched her, she would probably vanish. So he just stood and stared.

"Did you get Mac an appointment?"

How prosaic for a phantom to say something like that. She should declare her undying love, or she should give him a quest, or she should—

"Are you clicking on all your cylinders? What's the matter with you?"

That didn't sound at all like a dream.

"Carrie?"

"Who else could I be?"

He was so serious. "A phantom? What are you doing here?"

She could see that he was surprised. She took a deep breath, wondering if he was actually worth all the trouble he had become. She then asked patiently, "Did you call the doctor about Mac? You didn't call that woman, did you."

It wasn't even a question. So Stefan said, "No. I called Roger. He's going to work—"

"You called Roger's office? And you talked to Phyllis!"

"Why, yes. She's his nurse."

Impatiently, Carrie guessed, "And *she* said for you to come right over, until she realized it wasn't you she could strip naked."

"Why...Carrie!" Stefan was shocked. Was she jealous? She *sounded* jealous. His poor, shy, injured libido loosened and began to heal. He pushed it, "How could you be so hard on a good nurse like Phyllis?"

"When is Mac supposed to go over there?"

"Tomorrow."

"I'll come by for him."

Stefan questioned, "You want to see Roger?"

"No. I want that stupid nurse to let *Mac* see Roger. If I don't go and you do, she'll grab you and strip you bare before she realizes it's Mac who needs the help. Then she'll give him two aspirin and tell him to run along, that she has to give you an injection."

Beginning to enjoy the situation, Stefan slid his hands into his pockets and asked, "What sort of injection?"

She started, "The kind— Stefan, are you feeling ill?"

"Decaying for lack of attention."

She laughed very rudely. She waved her hand in a disbelieving gesture. She turned and stalked off to the house, calling, "Mac? Where are you?"

Stefan stood pensively in his untamed yard and considered that Mac feeling poorly was what had drawn the witch over to his house. Stefan tilted his head back and considered. He'd take a slug of— Naw, that wouldn't be romantic. He needed Mac's deterioration. But he realized he was too young to cope with untreatable old age.

Poor Mac.

He went into his own house to find Carrie on the phone. "Right away. No. It sounds very clogged." She looked right at Stefan and said, "I can't believe Stefan didn't know before today. Yes. I'll get him ready. Hustle up."

Stefan had taken his hands from his pockets and alarm shivered his body. "What's going on?"

"Mac has pneumonia."

"What!"

Her dramatic brown eyes came to him accusingly. "Couldn't you hear it?"

Stefan looked at Mac, who was sitting in the chair with his eyes closed. He opened one eye and smiled just a tad before he closed it again.

Stefan was stunned. Was the old man kidding?

But the slight, wheezing cough was rattly and harsh. Stefan became even more still.

Carrie asked, "Does Mac have a robe?"

"I'll see."

She called after him as he went quickly up the stairs two at a time... the way Carrie was supposed to've come to his own deathbed. She yelled, "A clean one!"

Mac called in a rough, clogged voice, "In the left-hand middle drawer."

Stefan suddenly realized this was serious. Mac was so sick, he was willing to go to the hospital! Mac! The iron man. Stefan's stomach got scared.

Scared? Over that old nuisance? How amazing. The guy was precious to Stefan? How astonishing. Why hadn't he realized it? He'd been so boggled by Carrie, he hadn't noticed anybody else.

His affection for the old coot had just sneaked into his feelings that Carrie had dominated so Stefan didn't even notice the concern for that old man? Hmm. Who else was he neglecting because of his concentration on that indifferent woman?

Himself. Well, no. He'd thought with kindly sympathy on all his own reactions and feelings. He'd been so concerned with himself that he hadn't noticed the old man was sick. Terrible. Terrible.

But there was that sly peeping eye and that slight smile Mac had given Stefan. Was he funning? Was he pretending he was that sick to get Carrie over there for Stefan Szysko? Was Mac that clever? Maybe he was just a chronic, clogged-lung man?

They'd better make sure.

Even if this was a clever hoax by that old man, he was trying to get Carrie concerned and therefore around Stefan. At least she would be available and not off somewheres with Pepper. Mac was trying. Stefan would help.

The ambulance came.

It was interesting to see how many of the Blinkers knew Mac and had become fond of him. The ambulance men all knew him and chuffed at him as they came into the house, blocking the door open and carrying in the stretcher.

They filled the house with their maleness just like Stefan's brothers did. They could do anything. Their confidence exuded from them. They were there.

They chaffed at Mac, complaining what a load he'd be as they gently eased him onto the stretcher and wrapped him. They carried him to the ambulance, telling him, "You're lucky we have a room for an old coot like you. Boy, you're heavy. What's Stefan been feeding you?"

They said, "Roger's a good doctor. He'll get you fixed up and back to monitoring Stefan's morals by tomorrow or even maybe next week, if there's a real pretty nurse there."

Another said offhandedly, "You'll probably get Bud. The nurses already know what a flirt you are and they're so giggly the doctors'll probably make Bud take care of you."

And the other guy said, "Yeah. Bud'll get you out soonest. He's ham-handed. He gives a man an enema like the guy's a shark!"

With all the chatter, the guys were gentle and careful and didn't even joggle the old man.

They asked Stefan, "You want to ride along?"

Stefan started to immediately get into the back of the ambulance, but Carrie pushed him aside as she said, "Bring my car to the hospital."

She said that just like he was some flunky. While she slapped the keys into his hand, she didn't flip a quarter at him.

And Stefan's libido shrunk down into a dried-up, pill-size nothing. She really didn't actually care about him. He would probably wither away into dust.

The only reason Stefan didn't panic and rush right away to the hospital was because of that sly, one-eyed glance from Mac and that tiny, asinine, wolfish-looking almost smile. If the old man was as sick as Carrie believed and had convinced the others, Mac would be sicker, wouldn't he?

Stefan felt more confident, then, about Mac; and he even went into the house and turned off lights and saw to it that the stove was off. Then he put her car off into the weeds to one side of the drive, got his own car and drove to the hospital.

He'd almost put her keys on the kitchen table, but he realized almost immediately that she could independently go to his house and retrieve them—and her car—without him knowing.

She was going to say to him that she had *told* him quite clearly that he was to drive her car to the hospital. He could say that in his concern for Mac he'd just forgotten about her car.

He pondered the fact that she would say something about it being over there in the weeds off the drive. Obviously, *some*body had moved it. And he'd say... uh... he—would—say—uh... he would tell her that she'd courteously put it there when she'd arrived. She would probably deny it. He'd be amazed she didn't remember.

When he reached the little hospital, people were running around and everyone was busy. Carrie was on one phone. She was calling her daddy to go get something from Fredricksburg? What was she doing telling her dad to do something from a hospital phone?

Gradually Stefan learned that Mac was really sick. They were kind and concerned and they weren't casual. They were so gentle.

Since Mac didn't have any family alive and he was staying with Stefan, Stefan was all the "family" Mac had. Stefan said he'd be responsible for Mac, so Stefan got family privileges. He could go into the hall and stand in Mac's doorway and talk at him through the face mask the nurses made Stefan wear.

For once, Mac couldn't reply. He lay with his bed tilted, with oxygen, with other tubes and monitors. And he would have nurses around the clock.

Everybody wore masks.

When Stefan went home in the middle of the first night, he was in bed before he understood the niggling flaw he'd noticed and not paid it any immediate attention.

With the keys now on his dresser, her car had been gone. She had another set of keys. She hadn't needed him to get her car back. She was a damned independent woman, capable of taking care of herself. She didn't need Stefan.

He faced the fact that no other woman would ever interest him, and it would be unkind to snag another woman when he still loved Carrie. He was doomed to live out his life without her.

He, too, sank into a sublevel existence, just like Mac.

* * *

The days passed, and Mac hovered. It was as if his spirit was already gone and only the discarded shell was there.

Just about the whole town came to see Mac. They dribbled in several at a time. Pat and Jerry flew in while the wild-driving Donna came in separately. Those people, like others, came in several times.

For a news spot, Pat used some of the original tapes of the old man; then Mac was shown in the hospital connected up with all those tubes. Pat filmed the town's concern.

So did Carrie's station. Carrie was at the hospital. She was serious. She occasionally slid her eyes sideways and watched Stefan, who had obviously given up all hope. He returned her car keys. She took them.

Manny would come by and report to Stefan on the doings at the car lot, at the dealership. Manny could put on a mask and stand in Mac's door and tell the silent hulk of the outrageous things people said about his "abandoned" Jeep impaled on the pole. And Manny'd tell the comments of passing motorists who'd driven Jeeps and loved them and couldn't believe anyone would give one up.

It was all on TV news stations and people wrote and came by. Mostly World War II men. They were especially supportive of a lonely veteran who had no kin left in the world.

He had Stefan.

With respiratory problems, there was no way any of the flowers could be put in Mac's room, so Carrie directed the volunteers to putting flowers in other rooms, sending them to shut-ins, then sending them to the schools.

The mail and flowers made the TV news and the newspapers. That, too, was picked up by the larger stations. And people began to send money to the old, ailing soldier, who had no family left and who'd defended our shores in a good war.

Because of Mac's age, they allowed his body to decide which way it wanted to be. Alive or gone. They kept him comfortable, turned him, monitored him and kept him clean and fed.

When Mac's decision came to live, he moved and coughed rather hard. That made them all smile. A hard cough. It wasn't anything heralding, but it was positive.

When Mac finally really opened his eyes, the first one he saw was Stefan, leaning in the doorway of a strange room and wearing a surgical mask. Stefan was complaining what a lazy, do-nothing man Mac was to lie in bed all day being waited on.

So the first sound Mac made was a "Humph!" of disagreement.

Stefan straightened, and his cheeks smiled over the top of the mask as his eyes misted. He said, "You old warthog."

And Mac asked in a gravely rough voice, "What the hell happened?"

"How come you didn't mention you weren't feeling good?"

Mac's words were rough but lazy from the dripping liquid still going into him. "You was in the doldrums. I couldn't give you any more grief."

"If you'd mentioned it then, you'd have saved us all a whole lot of effort. You're a nuisance." Stefan said that, but his voice was tender and his movements gentle. "You want for anything?"

"What're the nurses like?"

"You're getting well."

Mac laughed, but it made him cough. A nurse breezed in the way they walk at full pace, and she said to Mac, "We love hearing that, turn your head and do it some more."

Mac looked at her and widened his eyes. "I've died and gone to heaven? You're an angel? Does God know I got in?"

The black-haired nurse was used to men. She replied, "No, you old reprobate, you're still here with the rest of us."

And predictably, Mac then asked, "You a sinner?" And he smiled with all his wrinkles.

She sassed, "I've reformed."

"Well, darn."

Stefan still stood in the doorway, watching, listening, smiling. He couldn't ever remember feeling this lightened before in all his life. He'd given up on the old man. His house had been so empty. He'd never before felt so alone as he had when he left his vigil and went back to the empty house to get some sleep.

The nurses allowed Stefan to stay where he was while they checked Mac and rearranged him and smoothed his bed and fussed over him, teasing him.

It wasn't long before another of the nurses told Stefan that he ought to go home and sleep for a while. Mac was fine. He'd made it. He needed rest. The doctor would be by soon and check Mac out. This was a good time for Stefan to rest. The crisis was past.

Stefan listened stolidly. He hadn't realized how tired he was. It was as if he'd been running uphill for days, and he'd finally made it. How strange.

He went to Mac's door once more to look in. He said "I'll be back," to Mac, who lifted his hand! That just about unmanned Stefan. He turned and left the hospital, grinning at the exuberant nurses and staff. Lifting his hand and calling, "Thanks!" to them all.

He drove home in a fog of exhaustion, of emotion, over that old ragtag, intrusive nuisance of a man. Yeah.

He drove into his silent, empty driveway and stopped. Feeling as if he couldn't possibly be that tired, he got out of his car and closed the door. He went up the back steps and into his empty house.

Inside, the house was pristine. He walked around, looking at it as if it was real. There were some of Mac's overload of continuing flowers on the kitchen table, on the dining-room table, in the living room. The flowers really made the house look nice. It had never occurred to him that a house needs flowers.

Who had been so thoughtful?

He went upstairs, unbuttoning his shirt. He desperately needed sleep. And he looked into Mac's room. It was perfect. The bedding was clean. Everything had been put away.

Considering how kind someone had been, he went into his own room, which had been tidied and cleaned within an inch of its life—and he understood who had done it all.

His little black book was in the middle of his neatly made-up bed. Um-huh.

His clothes were all washed and ironed. His ironed handkerchiefs were stacked and whiter than they'd ever been since he left home.

And there were flowers in his room. It changed the room. It had only been a place to sleep before then. Now it was pretty. And he saw that the curtains were clean.

Had Carrie really done all this work? And again his eyes fell on the black book in the middle of the bed.

Had she been searching for it and decided she might just as well clean the place while she looked? Or had she cleaned the place first and *then* found the book?

Why had she put it there? It seemed to Stefan that she was saying, "I found it and I don't care."

He'd felt that way for quite a while. It only confirmed what he'd thought for some time. She was through with him.

He showered by rote, dried himself off and slid into the pristine bed. He slept so hard that he didn't dream.

And he wakened in the middle of the night. He got up, put on a pair of pajama bottoms and went downstairs to the kitchen. He turned on the light, and it was two in the morning.

He opened the refrigerator and found it, too, had been cleaned. And there were casseroles of interesting foods. He took one out and saw that it was from his mother.

That was normal. She did that on occasion. He looked at the others. They were from friends and sisters-in-law. Good people.

He chose one, nuked it and sat down to eat one vegetable-and-slivered-roast-beef combination. He drank from a glass of milk. He sliced a portion of pecan pie and had another glass of milk.

He sat with a contented stomach that was glad he'd finally realized he was hungry. He sighed, put his dishes in the empty dishwasher...it was empty! He didn't give it another thought, but went upstairs and back to bed . . . to sleep.

He dreamed Carrie confronted him angrily about the black book. He kept saying, "Why do you care?

You gave up on me." And she spat words at him that he couldn't understand.

In just two more days, the doctor had ordered Mac to be released from all the monitoring equipment. Mac could turn over and cough and snore marvelously. The nurses said he had a great snore. He offered to sleep with them so they would feel safe. They hooted.

Mac had so much attention that Stefan was a little jealous. He was quieter. He looked at the world without "seeing" it. He did what he had to do, and he slept, dreaming of an unattainable Carrie.

Mac came home. Stefan got him in his car and drove him home. Stefan had bought a pull-out couch so that Mac could sleep downstairs for a couple of days and not have to climb the stairs. There was a half bath off the back hall.

And the two were again sharing the house. Company came. Casseroles were spaced out and organized so they didn't have to cook. The two weren't aware that Carrie and Mrs. Szyszko had organized the donors.

It seemed everybody in the area came by Stefan's house to see Mac. The pinochle players were great help and underfoot most of the time.

Carrie came by often but never alone. But Mac said that she'd come alone once. Stefan hadn't been there. He'd gone out to his car lot to see if everything was all right.

Manny was confident and easy. He'd gained great confidence being alone and in charge. He whipped out a cloth and wiped a fender needlessly.

Stefan smiled. He said, "How about you becoming a junior partner and running a branch of our business over in Fredricksburg?"

Manny's mouth fell open and he just stared. Then he swallowed and he grinned. He nodded.

"How'm I gonna replace you here?"

And Manny straightened and said, "Rual's boy is interested, and he's good with cars. He can even fix them. Hire him to fix them, and let him come up from there."

"Good thinking."

"I can't believe this." Manny's grin stayed wide.

"You've earned it. Thank you for being around when I needed you. You did a great job. We need to go over and look around for the right place."

"I do have a suggestion."

"You do?"

"I thought we'd get to it some time and I've been keeping an eye out."

"Why didn't you mention it?"

"I wasn't a junior partner then."

The phone rang. It was Mac. He said, "Carrie called. Pepper is holding her up on the mountain. He's woman-napped her."

"No!"

Ten

Stefan hung up the phone and said, "Pepper has Carrie."

Manny asked, "What's that mean?"

"He's taken her up on the mountain."

"What mountain?" Manny frowned.

"The one north of town." It was just a craggy, difficult hill, but they called it a mountain. "I've got to go get Carrie."

"Her daddy'll do that," Manny protested. "Let him."

"No."

Manny was a man. "I'll go along."

"No. You wait here by the phone. I might need help. I have the car phone. Pepper has a tricky mind. I can't believe he'd woman-nap Carrie. Even him! It's not logical. But, you know, he must have. She wouldn't have called Mac and said that."

The phone rang again, and Stefan snatched it up.
"Yeah?"

Mac said, "I just called the Martindills, over by the
hill road? And it's blocked. You can't use the Jeep.
The only way up there is by horse."

"Horse!" He was allergic to horses. "Surely there's
another way. I'll call Joe. He'll know."

By the time Stefan looked up Joe's number, his line
was busy. It stayed busy.

With Pepper holding Carrie, time was of the es-
sence. Stefan needed to get there and protect Carrie.
What a surprisingly stupid thing for Pepper to do! The
guy was off his rocker! Stefan had never heard of
anything that stupid.

Manny said, "A Jeep can go anywhere a horse
can."

"Not our mountain. I've dumped two, trying off-
road. I'll have to find a horse." Fortunately, he had his
Stetson hat, and he always wore boots. Most TEX-
ANS are always prepared for anything. He took his
gun belt out of the safe and hung it around his hips,
settling it.

He called the Overmanns and was relayed by their
remote to Kirt. "Hey, Kirt, this is an emergency. Can
you lend me a horse?"

"Sure? How come?" Kirt asked.

"I have an errand to run," Stefan replied. "I'll tell
you all about it later."

"Well, sure. Glad to help out. Come on out."

Tersely, Stefan hung up the phone as he said to
Manny, "Be careful. Pepper might be luring me away
to destroy this place." Stefan got up and strode off
toward his car.

Manny's voice squeaked up in disbelief, "Pepper?
He wouldn't do anything like that."

Stefan stopped to emphasize the importance of what he said in a deadly serious manner, "If he'd snatch Carrie, he wouldn't think twice about trashing this place."

"I can't believe this!"

"Get Tad and the dog here to help you." Tad was the night man.

"Stefan . . ."

But Stefan had ducked into his car and roared off.

He got to Kirt's, and the horse was saddled and waiting. Stefan could see that. He turned his car off the track over under a mesquite. He got out and said, "Thanks, Kirt. I appreciate this."

Not surprisingly, Kirt asked, "What's going on?"

"I'll explain later."

Stefan had spent so much time out at Overmanns' refixing so many Jeeps, that he felt no obligation at all in borrowing a . . . horse.

He resettled his Stetson, took the reins and climbed on smoothly. He knew how to ride. And he did it well.

Kirt was saying, "Where ya going?" And he protested, "What the hell's going on?"

"I haven't time right now to chat. I'll be in touch. Leave my car alone." That last comment was very telling. Kirt was expert in lousing up a car's innards. Since it wasn't his own car, maybe he'd leave Stefan's alone.

And Stefan urged the horse forward immediately into a gallop, but he heard Kirt say, "Why do you need the horse? I can—"

But Stefan was gone.

As long as they were running, the smell of the horse wasn't too bad, but when they began to climb and had to go more carefully, the sweat and dander from the horse began to rise, and Stefan sneezed. The sound surprised the horse, which jumped and waggled his head, making the rein's rings jangle nicely.

How like that animal, Pepper, to snatch an unwilling female and take her off into oblivion.

It was exactly what Stefan had wanted to do any number of times with Carrie. How come Pepper was smarter than him? Damn.

Even if he was too late to save her from Pepper's greed, Stefan would take Carrie away from him and keep her for a while to himself. As long as one man had already woman-napped her, one more wouldn't traumatize her. She was so damned stubborn and difficult. Well, he'd see if she was upset and reluctant, and if she was neither, then he'd see if she minded.

Of course, first he would wring Pepper's neck.

Uhh. *Could* he wring Pepper's neck?

It was too late to consider the consequences. A man did as he had to do. No woman should have to tolerate a pushy man.

However... she'd danced close up with Pepper... and they'd talked earnestly at the dance. Had Pepper been coaxing her, then? He had appeared to be acting reasonable with her. Logical. Pepper was a logical man.

And she hadn't been leery of Pepper, as she'd danced close—

Stefan sneezed harshly, and the horse bolted. Damned, no-good, skittish horse.

Stefan allowed him to run a while and then quietened him down and got back to the trail and up onto the mostly mesquite-covered mountain.

As they got higher, he could see down below to the spilled truck, which had strewn winter wheat onto the road. The ant-men who swarmed around it would be a while getting it cleared. He looked up the way. The road was vacant.

He turned the horse onto the road and began the last of the earnest climb. Even cars took this section seriously.

The horse wasn't bothered. It looked around, but it jumped and threatened to bolt every time Stefan sneezed.

His eyes started to swell and his nose ran. Women were a nuisance. What was Stefan Szyszko doing riding a horse up a nasty road on this peculiar errand? Actually, Stefan knew Pepper was not going to kill or maim Carrie. He'd just taken her somewhere to have her alone.

Carrie hadn't treated Stefan very well lately. She'd been snippy and unfriendly.

The state police had search-and-rescue squads who went into any problem, so why hadn't Mac called them instead of him?

She'd cleaned his whole, entire house for him and Mac—and she'd put Stefan's little black book in the middle of his freshly made-up bed. She'd undoubtedly read the whole book and memorized or copied the names and phone numbers, and she'd probably call all those women and ask, "How was he?"

She knew.

She'd made love with him. Carrie Pierce had made love with Stefan Szyszko. He had been her first. That ought to count for something.

And Stefan Szyszko loved that blasted, no-account, ornery woman. That's why he was on that asinine horse and riding up that impossible hill to save her. When he found her he was going to shake her until her teeth rattled. Right after he broke Pepper's jaw.

Pepper was in pretty good shape.

He cultivated a fetish of being fit. He boxed. He was really pretty good. When that bunch from the Rio Grande valley came up to his place and started revving the motors and slamming around, Pepper was the one who convinced them to bug off.

Pepper tackled only one of them, but he'd chosen the right one to take out. Stefan and Manny had only to shoulder the other two. Then Pepper'd helped the guy to his feet and looked at his eye. Pepper had whistled and moved his head impressed. "You're gonna have a beauty."

How like Pepper to give a guy a black eye and then be impressed. Like he'd given the guy a trophy.

By then, Stefan's own eyes were almost closed with the allergic reaction to the horse. Especially Stefan's right eye. Pretty soon now, he would hardly be able to tell if his eyes were closed by Pepper or the horse.

As he topped the rise, to Stefan's surprise, he spotted Pepper's car almost instantly. And it was by the little shack that was called Look Out Point. People did come up there to "look out"—and make out and fool around and drink a lot of beer.

What had Pepper done to Carrie?

Being smart and having watched just about all the westerns ever filmed, Stefan looked around.

The top of the hill was bare of trees. You could see a long way away. It was pretty.

There were no other cars up there. If Pepper had any back up, they'd come by bus and it had left. That empty bus zipping back down the hill was probably what had overturned the wheat truck.

Stefan realized he'd probably lose this fight. The chair that would be swung at him wouldn't be a balsawood breakaway movie one. He faced the fact that he would be hurt.

Nobody would actually kill him. He knew that. Pepper wouldn't allow him to be killed. But he might take some pleasure in roughing Stefan up.

A man does as a man has to do.

Stefan approached the shelter with craft, riding carefully up from behind the closed-in rest rooms. He couldn't entirely blanket the sneezes, but he tried.

He dismounted and put the reins over the horse's head to trail and indicate the horse was to stay there. There was no rail to tie him to. Right around there were no trees or bushes. Nothing. The horse had to just stay. He said to this jumpy horse, "Stay." His voice was firm. With the circumstances, it pleased Stefan that his voice didn't waver.

The horse looked at him and then looked around. Then it walked to the side of the shelter that was shady and watched around.

Stefan took a deep breath of courage and sneezed enough to blow out all his brains. Not a subtle approach.

He went to the shelter and couldn't see inside because the TEXAS sunshine was too bright to see into the shadows. Knowing he was a target, he put his hand on his gun handle and stepped inside.

He sneezed again, about blowing himself back out.

Carrie's voice asked, "Stefan?"

She was there. That fragile, plaintive little voice was hers! What all had Pepper done to her to make her that vulnerable?

Stefan came into the shade enough, and his eyes began to adjust. There were three people at the table. Carrie was rising from her chair. Those seated were another woman . . . Trisha Overmann and Pepper.

Stefan's eyes riveted to Pepper. He was embarrassed to be caught and he . . . he was looking at the cards in his hands, then he glanced up at Stefan and asked, "Business slow?"

Carrie came over to Stefan, and she frowned at him. She reached up and put her hand on his face and peered under the brim of his Stetson. "What have you done to yourself? You're a *mess!*"

Just what every rescuer of women wanted to hear.

Stefan was a little terse. "Mac said Pepper hijacked you."

Pepper exclaimed, "Mac said—*what!*"

And the jolly three in the shelter burst into hilarious laughter. They had to lean over and slap the table or their knees and they hoooo-haaaa-ed.

In real TEXAS style, Stefan replied quite seriously but with courtesy, "Since there's no need for a rescue, I'll just go on along."

He turned with dignity, and took one step...

Still laughing, Carrie wrapped her arms around him and said, "No."

She was so soft.

Pepper exclaimed, "My God, man, you brought a *gun?* Was you gonna shoot *me?*"

Stefan replied stonily. "Or your gang."

That set the three off again.

Stefan sneezed.

Carrie asked, "Why are you sneezing? How'd you get up here? We're stuck by that truck overturned at the bottom of the road. Is it cleared away already?"

"No." Through the slits of his swollen eyes, Cisco saw her earnest, serious concern.

Looking very seriously at him, she said, "You came on a horse." A statement. She knew he loved her. She wrapped her arms around him, pinning his arms as she leaned against him, and she said a very soft, "Oh, Stefan."

He asked, "You didn't tell Mac you were being held?"

She looked up at Stefan in all innocence and frowned a little. "He said that?"

"Yeah."

That set the three off again into laughter. "That old coot!"

Stefan still wasn't amused. He asked, "What exactly did you say?"

"That I wouldn't be able to bring lunch to him. That Martla would instead. The truck had overturned and we'd be here a while."

So, of course, Stefan asked, "Why are you here?"

She shrugged. "We were plotting."

"What?"

She smiled. "How I could attract your attention."

Stefan closed the slits of his eyes, which was effortless since they were so swollen anyway. He sighed gustily and sneezed remarkably. He could finally say, "All's you needed to do was mention it. But instead, you scared the hell out of me."

Pepper was serious. "I was here. There wasn't any danger."

Deadly, Stefan replied, "I thought you'd snatched her and I'd have to—discipline you."

Pepper's eyes glittered with humor and challenge. "Think you could have?"

"No. I knew I'd lose."

"But you came anyway."

"I thought she needed me."

And Carrie said, "Oh, Stefan . . ."

Stefan looked back at her through the narrowing slits of his allergic eyes. He said, "I have to get the horse back."

Trisha volunteered, "Let me. I can ride down that mountain on anything."

But Stefan said, "My car's there at your place. I'll just go on down." And he walked out of the shelter.

Carrie trailed along. "Are you angry that I'm trying to catch you?"

"No. I feel like hell, and I want to get home."

"You were darling to come to help me. Thank you. Mac didn't mean any harm. He's just a natural-born matchmaker, and he knows that I love you."

"I'm not fit, right now, to convince you that I love you. I'll do that in another couple of days when I get over my latest entanglement."

"Latest— What do you mean!"

"This horse." He climbed on board, with the creak of leather and the slither of the reins. The horse waggled the bit in his mouth and moved his head. It was a good horse.

Stefan looked down on his love through blurry eyes a little regretfully. He'd wanted to be a hero, and he'd seemed foolish. It had been a useless quest. Mac had been earnest, trying to be helpful. Stefan looked down at his love and said, "Take care of yourself."

She squinted up at him and replied, "You know I always have."

"I'll be in touch."

"I'll look forward to it. And, Stefan, thank you from the bottom of my heart for coming here today on a horse this way. You are just the sweetest man."

He tipped his Stetson a tad and gallantly rode off, sneezing and controlling the reaction of the damned, jumpy horse.

When Stefan rode the horse in to Overmanns', Kirt came out. "What in hell happened to— Hey, I forgot. You're allergic to horses! Why'd you decide to do something this stupid?"

"It's a long story. You'll hear a dozen versions. I thought Carrie was marooned on the mountain."

Kirt's eye crinkles turned white with shock. "Then, you're in love with Carrie." It was a statement. "I can't tell you how sorry I am one of mine didn't get you."

"That's one of the nicest things I've ever heard, Kirt. And I had no choice in the matter. Carrie just stuck in my heart. She blinded me to the jewels you have as daughters. Carrie's blinded me to any other woman."

"That's so well said, I grieve more than ever we didn't get you."

"Ah, Kirt—" And he sneezed again. "Thank you for lending me this horse. Other than my allergy, he's perfect. A good horse. I've never ridden one better."

"I'll be in the doldrums over losing you as a son-in-law." Rather pensively, Kirt added, "Take care of yourself. I just may adopt you as a son."

"Talk to my daddy." While Stefan was touched by the sentiment, he was also aware of how many times he'd refixed the Jeeps Kirt had.

With his parting words of thanks, Stefan got into his car and drove away, knowing he'd have to vacuum it and leave the doors open to air out and to get rid of the horse dander from his clothing.

He got to his house and stood in the backyard, stripping off all his clothing to be washed and cleaned. He set his boots and hat in the garage. He rinsed in the hose then walked, naked, into his house to find it empty.

There was a note on the kitchen table. It was from Mac. It said, "To avoid a confrontation, I'm leaving for a few days' visit to Jerry's. I'll be back after a while. Mac.''

So the old coot knew what he'd done.

Stefan went in and showered. He found pills in the medicine cabinet that he hadn't had to take in some time. He called Manny and canceled the alert. Stefan said he'd come out if he was needed.

Manny explained, "I can handle it. Was Pepper really a threat?''

"No, it was all Mac. He's a matchmaker.''

Manny laughed unduly.

After Stefan hung up the phone, he dressed in jeans and a shirt. He put on moccasins and stood around. He could mow the yard, but after his encounter with the horse, there was no reason to push his allergy problem.

The pills' relief was gradual, but it came. His eyes weren't so swollen, and he'd quit sneezing. His head began to lighten.

He wondered how long it would be before Pepper quit teasing him about Carrie's rescue. And he decided it was worth it. He'd found that Carrie really loved him. She was serious. So was he. He'd just proven it to about everybody in Blink. By now, there couldn't be too many people who hadn't heard the story Pepper would tell.

But he still didn't know why Carrie and Pepper had been so seriously involved at that last dance. She'd said she was using Pepper to find a way to snare him. She had wanted Stefan Szyszko the entire time? Then why hadn't she come back to his house and shown him she loved him?

He'd've helped.

And he finally understood. She wanted permanence. She wanted him, but she felt overly bold to've been with him so intimately when he wasn't really committed.

He was a fool to dally when she was so precious. He needed to seal her up. He had felt that way all along. But he hadn't figured to get married quite so soon. There was some lure in forbidden fruit. And his taste of her had been heady.

He fingered his great-grandmother's ring, which hung in his ear. Yeah. He remembered when his great-grandmother lay dying and told him that he might like to give that ring to his wife when he had one. She'd said it was pure gold. If he didn't want the actual ring, then maybe he could have the gold melted down and made into something for himself.

He'd worn it on his hand when he was nineteen, but then women thought it was a marriage ring of some kind. So he'd had it cut open and a catch fixed onto it so that he could wear it in his ear. It had caused comment.

Since his daddy had shipped him out to the gulf for his junior year in college, the year most students are restless, the earring had been appropriate. He'd claimed to've been on a pirate ship that year, and the ring in his ear had made his pirate story plausible.

He tenderly felt the ring and knew he would have eventually given it to Carrie. He'd do it now. He'd talk to her father that very night. He'd do this right.

But she came over to his house about five-thirty. She came busily up the back stairs, carrying a basket. She greeted him rather shyly, but she smiled with her blush. She went into his kitchen and emptied the basket. In it was a salad and two steaks, which she put into the refrigerator. There were two baked potatoes. Sour cream. A bottle of wine. Rolls. A coconut-cream pie.

He grinned, standing there, his eyes almost fully open again. He looked at her tenderly.

Enunciating carefully, and still pink-faced, she told him, "I'm spending the night with...Mary Lou." And she gave him a very precious and innocent look.

He sobered.

She took out a toothbrush from the picnic basket, and holding it up in front of her, she asked with wide, innocent eyes, "Where shall I put this?"

His heart just about stopped altogether. He replied, "You're going to spend the night with...me?"

She shrugged and just grinned at him, her cheeks scarlet.

Stefan eased over to see what else was in that basket. And it was empty.

She had no nightclothes with her?

She expected to sleep naked in his bed and have... him...keep her warm?

His breathing picked up and his eyes on her were innocent and greedy at the same time. He asked, "Are you getting committed to me?"

She was open about it and told him, "I have been all along. I just need something like that from you. I need to know you're serious about me."

"I am."

"I can't move in with you and let you play around with me and not be committed."

"I'm gonna talk to your daddy this week. Not tonight."

"You've decided?"

"You know that. Why else do you think I came clear up on that mountain to find you and rescue you."

"That's what convinced me to come over here tonight. You're so darling."

"You've been a handful lately."

She tilted up her chin. "You haven't been close enough to get a handful of me."

"Sassy women get in trouble."

"I didn't know that. Are you still deciding if I can stay with you? You haven't told me where to put my toothbrush." She smiled.

"Upstairs in my bathroom there's an empty notch in the cabinet?"

And she turned prissily around and went out of the kitchen. He heard as she went delicately up the stairs—very different from Mac's thuds—and her soft steps went over into his bathroom.

Suddenly his mind went frantically around as to what reading material might have been left there…and what was in the cabinet. . . .

She came downstairs and stood, blushing, smiling at him. Committed to him.

She was so precious. He was boggled. He told her, "I'm not hungry right now. Not for food."

She agreed. "I had a late lunch."

He picked her up and carried her from the kitchen, through the dining room, into the hall and up the stairs.

Against him, her body felt different from the sack of grain. She was lighter. Her surface was sweet, and the length of her body was better, as was the distribution of her weight. She had her arms around his shoulders, helping.

Carrying her made him feel like a Roman soldier who captured a Sabine woman. He felt powerful and potent.

He took her to his bed. She wasn't surprised. She helped. He undressed her and looked at her curled naked on his bed. She had a delicate gold chain around her throat, and she had on a watch.

That was all.

No garter belt and no stockings.

The unveiled Carrie.

She sat up, curled into herself. One knee was bent up and the opposite arm lay on that knee, somewhat shielding her as she watched him. Her eyelids were heavy and her mouth was soft. Her cheeks were exceptionally pink.

She watched as he removed his own clothing. He knew he had her attention, so he did it for her. He had a good body. He was well made. He was a little embarrassed he was so triggered.

She murmured flattering sounds. His eyes brimmed humor, and he licked his lips as he smiled.

He sat on the side of the bed and squeezed together the ends of his great-grandmother's earring. The catch gave, and he removed the earring.

He got tweezers from the bathroom and broke off the little prongs that had been added, and he squeezed the soft old gold back into a circle. He lifted her hand, and the ring fit on her ring finger.

There were tears in her eyes as she looked up at him.

He leaned to kiss her soft lips with the gentleness of a complete commitment. He told her, "I love you."

She gasped with great emotion and put her arms around him as she said, "Oh, Stefan, I love you so."

Their lovemaking was gentle and sweet, and they prolonged it wondrously. They moved and gasped and wiggled and sighed. The rubbing of their hot bodies was marvelously sensual. They panted and groaned and gasped. Their climax was simultaneous on that momentous night, and that in itself was unique. Delicious. Wondrous. Perfect.

They lay in the lingering evening's light and smiled as they sighed and could think of nothing especially to say. Their contentment was lazy and their movements languorous.

When their empty, lied-about stomachs began to really growl from their borderline starvation, they rose from the bed. Stefan only put on jeans, and she wore his black Chinese silk robe.

He'd bought it in Dallas five years ago and had never worn it. Now he knew why. It was for her.

She watched his dark eyelashes cover his eyes as he turned back the sleeves. Her cheeks were not only pink from her remarkable adventure in a man's bedroom, they were somewhat abraded by his evening's whiskers.

He saw how he'd reddened her blushing surface as he carefully turned up the sleeves, leaning to kiss her as he did that. He said, "My God, Carrie, how could I have found you in a place called Blink?"

"Uhh." She looked off in great thought, knowing she had all of his attention, and supplied the reply, "You didn't . . . blink?"

He groaned, but he hugged her soft, silk-covered body to his and then he made purring sounds as he rubbed his whiskers into her throat and along her ear.

She mentioned, "I'm starving."

"I thought you had a late lunch?"

"How rude of you to remember I said that."

He leaned his head back to look into her eyes. "Why did you tell me you'd eaten your lunch late?"

Her glances were at everything but him, and she blushed really scarlet as she bit her smiling lips. "You know!"

"You wanted me."

She looked up, and her smile was getting out of control as her eyes spilled laughter. "How rude of you to guess!"

They almost went right back to bed then, but as he gave her his killer, brain-numbing kiss, her stomach growled in protest! Stefan was shocked. "Doesn't your daddy ever feed you?"

"Not today."

He pulled his head back a tad farther and looked at her with great, cautious mime. Then he asked carefully, "How much does it cost to feed a woman with such a pushy appetite?"

She shrugged so fascinatingly in his black silk robe that he forgot the question. Being an environmentalist and concerned with the survival of all creatures, he automatically knew he had to feed this particularly special entity.

Together they fixed dinner. He did the steaks and put hers on first so they came off at the same time. She mixed the salad and saw to the potatoes and did the rolls just right.

They kissed and touched and smiled and smiled and smiled. Although he shaved with his battery razor, it was too late. Her face was already a mess, but he didn't cover it with the old stench of muscle soother men used to use. He smoothed aloe over her face, her neck, her shoulders, her breasts in slow, circular movements . . . and they went back to bed.

She whispered to him, *"Jocie kocham."* And his recovered eyes filled with moisture.

Mac didn't seem surprised when the couple told him they would be married. Mac didn't even congratulate them. He just said, "You gotta know you'll never get rid of me?"

That was when they realized they'd known that for some time. So they just nodded.

All the Szyszkos and the Pierces got together and spent a weekend building a bachelor apartment for Mac off the back screened porch. There was no other way to do it. Mac was already settled in, a whole lot like a battle-scarred tomcat that has chosen to stay.

The pinochle games continued through the years, and the old men laughed and visited there with Mac.

Stefan's and Carrie's children were a lot like them in that they were stubborn and interesting and individual. The parents were a pair, a couple, and they lived happily ever after, quarreling a little, laughing a lot and sharing.

* * * * *

Get Ready to be Swept Away by
Silhouette's Spring Collection

Abduction
& Seduction

These passion-filled stories explore both the dangerous
desires of men and the seductive powers of women.
Written by three of our most celebrated authors, they are
sure to capture your hearts.

Diana Palmer
Brings us a spin-off of her Long, Tall Texans series

Joan Johnston
Crafts a beguiling Western romance

Rebecca Brandewyne
New York Times bestselling author
makes a smashing contemporary debut

Available in March at your favorite retail outlet.

Take 4 bestselling love stories FREE

Plus get a FREE surprise gift!

SILHOUETTE®
Desire®

MAN of the **MAN** *Month* **N** 1995

Don't let the winter months get you down because the heat is about to get turned way up...with the sexiest hunks of 1995!

January: *A NUISANCE*
by Lass Small

February: *COWBOYS DON'T CRY*
by Anne McAllister

March: *THAT BURKE MAN*
the 75th Man of the Month
by Diana Palmer

April: *MR. EASY*
by Cait London

May: *MYSTERIOUS MOUNTAIN MAN*
by Annette Broadrick

June: *SINGLE DAD*
by Jennifer Greene

MAN OF THE MONTH...
ONLY FROM
SIILHOUETTE DESIRE

MOM95JJ-R

Also available by popular author

LASS SMALL

Silhouette Desire®

#05655	THE MOLLY Q	$2.75	☐
#05684	*TWAS THE NIGHT	$2.79	☐
#05697	DOMINIC	$2.89	☐
	The following titles are part of the Fabulous Brown Brothers miniseries		
#05830	A NEW YEAR	$2.99	☐
#05848	I'M GONNA GET YOU	$2.99	☐
#05731	A RESTLESS MAN	$2.89	☐
#05755	BEWARE OF WIDOWS	$2.89	☐
#05800	BALANCED	$2.99	☐
#05817	*TWEED	$2.99	☐
#05860	SALTY AND FELICIA	$2.99 U.S. $3.50 CAN.	☐
#05879	LEMON	$2.99 U.S. $3.50 CAN.	☐

*Man of the Month
(limited quantities available on certain titles)

TOTAL AMOUNT	$
POSTAGE & HANDLING	$
($1.00 for one book, 50¢ for each additional)	
APPLICABLE TAXES**	$_____
TOTAL PAYABLE	$_____
(check or money order—please do not send cash)	

To order, complete this form and send it, along with a check or money order for the total above, payable to Silhouette Books, to: **In the U.S.:** 3010 Walden Avenue, P.O. Box 9077, Buffalo, NY 14269-9077; **In Canada:** P.O. Box 636, Fort Erie, Ontario, L2A 5X3.

Name: _____

Address: _____ City: _____

State/Prov.: _____ Zip/Postal Code: _____

**New York residents remit applicable sales taxes.
Canadian residents remit applicable GST and provincial taxes.   SLSBACK4

Silhouette®
™